Wha
Christi

MW01488157

"In *Mysterious Ways*, novelist Terry Burns writes with an entertaining ease... Plot twists and surprises enter the story with regularity, and (for once) this is a suspense novel that doesn't have to resort to murder to keep the tension high. Easily recommended!"
--Mike Nappa, author of *Who Moved My Church?*

"[*To Keep A Promise*] is particularly excellent for young adults. ...easy to follow prose, the plot moves at a brisk pace and all strings are neatly tied up in the end. ...exciting action...Burns is at his best when he uses his descriptive talents to kernel the Christian message within this tale of the old West."
--Meredith Campbell, Midwest Book Reviews

"The many messages of how to live a satisfying Christian life permeate your Westerns. You do not preach. You do not proselytize. Your characters demonstrate how life can be lived by Christian principles. That, sir, is a literary gift."
Sally J. Walker, Editorial Director, The Fiction Works

"Of all the books of Terry Burns I've read, I would rate *Brothers Keeper* (available January 2006) to be his best book to date. ...filled with moments of humor and action that will keep the reader going until the surprising conclusion. Terry Burns has written another great book."
Les Williams, Freelance Reviewer

Terry Burns

Trails of the Dime Novel

Echelon Press

This is a work of fiction. Names, characters, places, and incidents are products of the author's imagination or are used fictitiously and are not to be construed as real. Any resemblance to actual events, locales, organizations, or persons, living or dead, is entirely coincidental.

Echelon Press Publishing
56 Sawyer Circle #354
Memphis, TN 38103

Copyright © 2005 by Terry Burns
ISBN: 1-59080-409-0
www.echelonpress.com

All rights reserved. No part of this book may be used or reproduced in any manner whatsoever without written permission, except in the case of brief quotations embodied in critical articles and reviews. For information address Echelon Press.

First Echelon Press paperback printing: February 2005
Cover Art © Nathalie Moore

Embark and all its logos are trademarks of Echelon Press.

Printed in Lavergne, TN, USA

Dedication

To the three cowboys that help keep me young, my youngest grandchildren; Bryce Burns, Alex Waters and Jaylen Gunter. I'm in no hurry for you boys to get old enough to read this.

Finally, I dedicate the book to Grandmother Tunnell, the Irish storyteller who passed the love of words down through my mother to me, telling me the stories several chapters were based on, and appearing as herself in the true story in Chapter 18.

This book is set in the late 1800s when a small publication existed, popularly known as the dime novel. They were small books, known for their florid language and generally wildly exaggerated tales. With a public starved for news from the West, the little tomes achieved an unrivaled popularity.

This is the story of a delightfully naïve young man on a quest to write the history of the West in this medium.

Some small latitude is taken with the dates to permit the telling of the stories in this manner, but all historical references are accurate and correct.

One:

The Daring Daylight Train Robbery

My name is no name for an adventure writer, Rick Dayton thought. *I need something strong, adventurous...manly. It has to be a name that* sounds *like action and excitement. It has to announce that I am someone who's seen it all, done it all, and spits in the very face of danger.*

He mulled it over for several minutes as he waited for his train. Then it hit him, "Texas Jack."

The lady on the bench next to him jumped as if she had been poked with a sharp stick. She turned wide eyes toward him and said, "Pardon?"

Rick removed his hat. "I'm sorry, I didn't mean to startle you, ma'am. I merely said, I'm Texas Jack, an author, and I'm on my way West to work on my new book."

She gave a small nod of acknowledgement. "How exciting."

He lifted his chin, basking in the glow of her attention. "Yes, it is, and dangerous, too, of course."

"Oh, my."

It suddenly occurred to him that he needed a pipe. To present the right image, an author should have a pipe. No, that's not exactly right, a cigar. A Western author should have an ever-present cigar. He thought it would make him look older, too.

Rick tipped his hat to the lady as he got up. "I'm sorry, ma'am, but as much as I'm enjoying your company, I find I am quite without a cigar. I wouldn't have smoked one in your presence without permission, of course, but even to be able to have it in one's mouth, unlit or not, can be a comfort. I need to get over to the shop and stock up before the train leaves."

Rick went to the tobacconists and purchased a couple of boxes of good Cuban cigars. Unable to wait, he immediately bit the end off one of the dark, tightly wrapped stogies, and lit it. The noxious smoke brought on a coughing fit and his eyes filled with tears. *Whew, these things are terrible.* He stubbed it out and thought perhaps he would simply chew on them in the corner of his mouth the way his city editor used to do.

The conductor shouted, "*Boooaaaaarrrrdddd!*" as Rick returned and found a seat. He made himself as comfortable as the hard, upholstered, straight-backed bench would allow, and opened the new leather-bound journal he had just purchased. He had determined that the slender volume would become his constant companion, diary, and repository of all the facts that would make up the writing he would soon be doing.

Eager to get started, Rick opened the letter that

had made this trip possible. It was from his Uncle Edgar. He read it again:

Dear Nephew,

If you are reading this it means I am dead. So be it. Don't waste time grieving for me, for I had a good life. You are my only surviving family, and as such, inherit my estate. You will find my will has an interesting condition, however, and it was my wish that you be given time alone to read this letter before the reading of the will.

You see, I know your dreams and your ambitions, but I also know you will never pursue them. You think you have a career going at that newspaper, and that could be true, but you are capable of much more. I see the potential. I'm aware of the flowery phrases your editor crosses out of the little stories he allows you write. I also know these phrases are the language of the small paperback novels now becoming so popular. You are a natural for them.

So, I leave you no choice. My will provides for you to receive a monthly stipend to cover your expenses as you travel, but to receive it you must write. If you don't, you will not receive a nickel. You might say I am reaching out from the great beyond to push the chick from the nest.

Some might criticize me for doing this to a twenty-two-year-old boy, but I think you are ready. After all, the West is full of young men your age, driving cattle, in the Army, and exploring the new frontier. That's where your future lies, I know it.

I wish you Godspeed, my young nephew. You were my most cherished companion while I was alive, and now that I am dead (you have no idea how it sounds to say that about myself), rest assured I shall look down on you to see how well my little plan succeeds.

Your Uncle Edgar

Rick missed him terribly. Uncle Edgar's death made him the last of his line, on his father's side. He still had family on his mother's side, one headed by the reigning matriarch, his maternal grandmother, but that was a different story entirely.

Rick could hardly overlook his good fortune. He had $200 in his pocket, which would normally represent several months of wages. The law firm of

Daggett, Crockett, and Allen had estimated such an amount would transport him West and cover his expenses for the first month. Future transactions would be handled through the fine facilities of the Western Union. Modern technology was indeed amazing.

Before Rick left town, he had exploited his newspaper connections, such as they were, to get in touch with a publisher. Hungry for material for the little adventure paperbacks, they were very interested in an author willing to pay his own expenses, and only requiring compensation *if* they published his work. They considered it a fine arrangement, indeed. Again, any further negotiations, legal or financial, were to be handled by Daggett, Crockett, and Allen.

He settled back in his seat, wondering what Uncle Edgar would say of him now, about him adopting a new name, even for the purpose of writing. Texas Jack! Yes, he liked that, but how about a last name? Jack what? "Texas Jack Hammer," he decided. *Yes, that's it. Now, there's a name with steel in it.* He tried it again.

"Texas Jack Hammer," he said, intense satisfaction on his face.

"Who is that?"

Rick looked up to find a large straw hat perched on a young girl's head. Under the brim of the hat, between two long braided pigtails, peered a pair of eyes that were a most remarkable shade of blue.

He straightened his backbone and adopted a rather condescending tone. "I beg your pardon?"

It didn't faze her in the least. "Who is Texas Jack Hammer?"

Rick took hold of his coat lapel with his left hand, sure it presented a very scholarly pose. "I am Texas Jack Hammer. I'm an author on my way West to write my next book."

Both hands gripped the top of the seat as she scrutinized him. "What's an author?"

"An author is someone who writes books."

The lady next to the girl spoke sharply, "Kasey, turn around and leave the gentleman alone."

Rick lifted his hat and turned his attention to the lady. "It's all right, madam. One cannot begin cultivating fans at too young an age."

Returning his attention to the girl, he said, "Do you read adventure stories?"

She shook her head so hard that it caused the pigtails to swing rapidly. They continued after she stopped her head. "I don't read at all, I'm only five."

"Well, perhaps when you begin to read, you'll start with one of mine."

Kasey gave him an appraising look, measuring him. "You don't look like someone named Texas Jack."

"And what should a Texas Jack look like?"

"He should have a big hat, and a scarf, and spurs, and a big gun."

It was Rick's turn to shake his head. "It's not a

scarf, it's a bandanna."

"What is?"

He waved the question aside. "Never mind, what you describe is a cowboy. I'm not a cowboy, I merely write about them."

"How can you write about them if you aren't one?"

"I'm not a horse either, but I write about them, too."

"Do you ride horses?"

Rick smiled. He had her here. "Of course, there's nothing I enjoy more than a good canter through the park."

"I don't think horses out here canter."

The lady spoke again. "Kasey, I said to turn around and sit down. You're annoying the gentleman." Reluctantly, the child did as she was told.

Rick concurred with the lady; she was an annoying child, impertinent actually. Still, her questions kept nagging at him. She was right, that was what bothered him the most. He couldn't write effectively about things without experiencing them, which was the reason for the trip.

Then there was the matter of his appearance. Perhaps the child had something there as well. Maybe his fans would expect a certain bravado in appearance, a dashing, Western oriented style of dress. He felt he shouldn't try to look like a cowboy, of course, but a Western hat might be in order, and of course boots, Western boots. He determined to get them at the earliest opportunity.

Yet, there was something Rick could do now, and he did. He removed his tie and threw it out the window. Acutely aware that he had a lot to learn about cowboys, he still felt totally certain they didn't wear ties. He resolved from this point on, neither would he...never again.

Rick watched the offending garment flutter away from the speeding train. He closed the window, and his reflection caught his eye. It held his attention. He looked like what he was, a bookworm. Tall and lean, ungainly at best, he was under no illusions about himself. It would be foolish to try and dress the part of a cowboy.

He looked over the top of his wire frame glasses at the man reflected in the window. *Let's not be ridiculous.*

Rick closed his eyes and sat back. He pictured himself in a flamboyant Western costume, riding a large black horse with fire in his eyes. He saw himself...

"Mr. Texas Jack?"

The image disappeared. The blue eyes were back.

"Yes."

"Do you have a gun?"

"I do not."

"Aren't you gonna need a gun where you're going?"

Rick pondered that one for a minute. He liked the sound of it. He could easily picture himself with cold steel swinging from his hip. He shook his head and dismissed it from his mind. Wearing a gun, without being proficient in its use, sounded like a good way to get killed.

The condescending tone came back into his voice. "One should only wear a gun if they are prepared to use it. I am not inclined to do so, so it would be foolish of me to put one on."

"You were sure right."

"Right about what?"

"You're not a cowboy."

"Are you an authority on the subject?"

"What's an authority?"

"Do you know about cowboys?"

"We have cowboys on our ranch."

"You have a ranch?"

"Not me, silly, but my daddy does. My horse Patches is there."

Oh, great. I've been lecturing this young lady about cowboys and she lives on a ranch. Rick pulled out his journal and made his first entry:

Interview Rule Number One: *Find out how knowledgeable any subject is before telling them your personal thoughts.*

Interview Rule Number Two: *Never take ANYBODY for granted.*

He underlined *anybody* three times.

Rick tucked the book back into his coat pocket and returned his attention to the girl. "So, how big is this ranch of yours?"

"Daddy says it isn't very big."

"You raise cows on it?"

"Yes."

"How many cows are on the ranch?"

"I don't know, I can't count past ten."

"Let me try it this way. Once you get back to the boundaries of your ranch, how long will it take to get to your house?"

"Oh, we won't have to camp out or anything, not if we get an early start."

Rick reached for the journal again without comment, and wrote: *Size in the West is relative.*

He replaced the journal in his pocket and continued what had now become an interview. "What do these cowboys do on your ranch?"

"They rope the cows, and brand the cows, and watch the cows, and kick the cows, and cuss the cows; mostly they do things with the cows. I guess that's why we call them cowboys."

"They cuss the cows in front of you?"

"Not if they know I'm there. If I'm there, they make talk with big holes in it, like, 'You...I'm gonna...you dirty...I'd like to...' They think I don't know what goes in the holes, but I do."

Kasey's companion awoke from her nap. "Kasey,

are you bothering the man again? I told you not to..."

Rick tipped his hat again and leaned forward. "Your daughter isn't bothering me, ma'am, really she isn't. As a matter of fact, she opened my eyes on a couple of things."

"Oh, she isn't my daughter, she's my sister, and I'm afraid she can be something of a pest if she puts her mind to it."

"Certainly not the case here. Ma'am, do you mind if I move to the seat facing you? I am traveling West, and your sister has given me to understand you have a ranch out there. As a writer, I would enjoy finding out more about it."

"I don't mind if you sit there. Ordinarily I would not engage in a conversation with a stranger, but I suppose one must make allowances on a public conveyance. It certainly would help pass the time."

"It is not necessary for us to remain strangers, ma'am." He moved around to the facing seat, bowed, and offered his hand. "I am Rick Dayton."

She took the hand, but had a puzzled expression on her face. "Rick? But I thought..."

"A pen name, ma'am. Many writers use them."

She smoothed out her skirt, obviously to keep from having to make eye contact. "I see. I am Shanda James, and this is my sister Kasey."

Rick sat. "Your sister and I are old friends by now." Rick pulled his glasses down with his forefinger, and peered over the top as he looked at the youngster.

"Even if I am not a cowboy."

He stored his valise under the facing seat, then looked up, prepared to exchange some opening pleasantries. The face he looked into removed all thoughts from his mind. Shanda was breathtaking.

Her beauty wasn't such that one would encounter on the Boston social scene, no lace and cosmetics here. No, she radiated a healthy glow, no doubt from being out in the sun on her ranch. Her eyes were a soft brown, hidden by long eyelashes. Her hair fell softly around her face. He found himself mesmerized, his jaw slack, and his eyes wide.

"Mr. Dayton, are you all right?"

He closed his mouth and tried to regain his senses. "Yes, why do you ask?"

"I don't know, you looked as if you had seen a ghost or something. You looked at me so..."

He cleared his throat, and pushed his glasses up more firmly. "I'm sorry, I didn't mean to be rude. You see, in order to write I have to be able to describe the people I meet. Please don't think me as trying to be familiar with you when I say this, but your beauty will be hard to express with mere words."

"Oh my." Her eyes widened for an instant before her gaze demurely dropped. "If you are going to carry on in such a manner, perhaps it's best you return to your seat."

"No, I'm sorry, I'll behave myself. Perhaps you'll understand what I mean if you helped me describe some of the other passengers. How about the gentleman across the aisle?"

She glanced at the other passenger. "A drummer. He's dressed like a banker, but doesn't wear the clothes as comfortably as a man of wealth would. The redness of his face suggests a fondness for drink. Yes, definitely in sales."

"Say, you're pretty good at this. How about the man across from him?" He recorded the description in his journal.

"A cowboy returning after letting the badger loose in the city."

"Letting the badger loose? What a delightful expression. I can guess what it means." He added the notation.

"Yes, I hear it used by the hands on our ranch. The red on his neck and hands made me think he might be a working hand, but when he removed his hat to me getting on and I saw the white line on his forehead where his hat topped, and that above his wrist under his cuff. Besides, he wears those dress clothes as if they had a hair lining. He can barely keep them on."

Rick made constant notes. She went on to describe many of the passengers, seeming to get enjoyment in the little diversion. She also told him a lot about their ranch, and what it was like to live on one. The ranch turned out to be in the hill country, northwest of Austin, Texas. While not considered large by Texas ranch standards, it was a size Rick could scarcely comprehend.

They dropped the formalities, and were soon laughing and joking. Kasey squealed as they were suddenly plunged into the darkness of a long tunnel. When they emerged, and Rick's eyes adjusted, he had to blink to make sure what he saw was real.

Two men stood at the head of the car with bandannas over their faces, guns in their hands. "Is entertainment scheduled on this trip?" Rick asked.

"You may find this entertaining," Shanda said, "but these men certainly aren't doing it for such a purpose. We're about to be robbed."

"Robbed! Surely not!" Rick looked around. The other passengers sat with their hands high in the air, the look of fear on each face unmistakable.

The hard-looking men wore nice-looking clothes, and seemed to be comfortable in them. They commanded the attention of the passengers, but at the same time weren't particularly aggressive or threatening. They fascinated Rick.

The nearest man spoke. "Everybody just keep those hands where we can see 'em. Jasper, you go skin those pokes."

"Skin those pokes?" Rick whispered.

"It means to take your wallet," Kasey answered.

Rick pulled out the journal to write down the phrase.

"Hey, you," the closest of the desperadoes said. "I said to keep your hands where I can see them."

Rick looked up. "Who, me?"

"I ain't talking to your Aunt Martha."

"Oh, that one's good! May I write it down?"

"What are you talking about?"

"I'm a writer. Oh, by the way, here's my money. I'm afraid I only have about $160 left, but you're welcome to it." He opened his coat. "As you can see, I'm not armed."

"You sure are happy about this. When we rob folks, they generally tend to resent it somewhat."

"Yeah," said the other outlaw, "most of them get pretty testy."

"That's because they are losing money, and I certainly understand how they feel. I, on the other hand, feel like I am making an investment of the money in a story which will bring me back more money than I am losing."

"You gonna write about us in this here story?"

"Of course."

"You fixin' to mention us by name?"

"That's up to you."

They looked at each other, "Can't see how it'd hurt. Who reads these books?"

"Most everybody," Rick lied.

"Well, the plain fact is you are being robbed by the famous James Gang. I'm Jesse, and that there is my cousin Jasper. My brother Frank is doing business up at the express car at the present time."

Rick looked at Shanda. "Is he related to you?"

"Not that I know of."

"What are you two jabbering about?" Jesse asked.

"Her last name is James. Her name is Shanda, and this is her sister Kasey. We were wondering if you might be related."

"Well, just in case you are kin, you can hold on to your valuables. I ain't robbing no kin-folks."

"If such is the case, may I point out that I *am* traveling with them?"

"Not on your life, dude, you done said you're making money on this deal. The way it sounds, you oughta be giving us more money than you are."

"That's probably true, maybe next time?"

A man burst in the door. "Jesse, what in blue blazes are you doing, having a tea party?"

"I'm getting my name in a book, Frank. This here guy's a writer."

"Are you crazy? Then they'll know it was us that did it."

"Now Frank, you know we get blamed for it whether we do it or not."

"Well, that's true. While you're at it, you want to sit here and talk to the Pinkerton Detectives, too? I'll bet they'd be happy to put your name in a book."

Rick wrote so fast that his pencil nearly started to smoke.

"Aw, ease up, Frank, maybe this guy will write something nice about us for a change."

"You gentlemen have certainly been most pleasant

to me," he said.

Frank said, "I don't get it. You ain't mad you've been robbed?"

"I'll tell you about that," Jesse said, "in fact, he says we got more coming later."

"It's called royalties," Rick nodded in affirmation.

"Yeah, well how about if we give you our address so you can send it to us," Frank said. "Or better yet, maybe we can put you on our mailing list along with the Pinkertons, and assorted sheriffs and marshals."

"Oh, yes, I see the problem. Well, perhaps we'll find a way to square it up in the future."

"I gotta say that's a first. I never robbed nobody before who offered to send more money later."

The conductor arranged to send a wire for Rick to Daggett, Crockett, and Allen with news of the robbery, and a request to wire money to be waiting at a stop down the line. The wire also promised a manuscript for his first book, tentatively entitled *The Daring Daylight Train Robbery*, to follow by post.

It turned out Shanda had been working as a public stenographer in New York, so on the rest of the trip she helped by taking dictation on the manuscript.

Rick dictated it in the heady prose that was the style of the publications:

"*Frank and Jesse James walked into the railroad car big as life*," he started.

"Frank was in the express car, remember?" Kasey

volunteered.

"It's called artistic license, Kasey. You can make changes in a true situation in order to make a story read better."

"So, it's all right to lie in a book?"

"It isn't a lie, it is within the spirit of what happened. It is merely packaging it for commercial consumption."

"Oh, I see," but it was clear she didn't.

Rick understood the rules for the little tomes. Everything had to be bigger than life. Men had to be of heroic proportions, women had to be always in peril, but never harmed or violated, and villains had to be magnificently evil with no redeeming qualities.

"Where was I? Oh yes. *Their cold black eyes were hard as the steel bars on the door as they glared from above the bandannas covering their faces.*"

Kasey looked over at the doors. No bars. She started to say something, but Shanda said, "*Shush.*"

"*The barrels of the six guns in their hands looked as big as railroad tunnels.*"

"They just had one gun, not two...oh, yes, I know...*shush.*"

"*In a cold voice that brooked no interference, Jesse said, 'Everybody put your hands up!', then had one of his men skin the pokes of the passengers. A little girl said, 'Daddy, what does skin a poke mean?' He told her it meant he was going to have his wallet taken.*"

"I didn't say that, you did. I know what skin a poke means." Kasey said, indignant.

"It's only a story."

"Well, I don't like it. You can lie if you want to and call it something else, but I don't like you lying about me. It makes it sound like I didn't know what skin a poke means. I *know* what it means."

"All right, all right! Make that a little boy asks his daddy."

Rick went on to dictate the entire story, punctuated with substantial editing from the opposite seat, and had a neatly handwritten manuscript to post when he stopped to pick up his money.

He stepped off the train and walked to the open window of the station. He sent the manuscript to his lawyers, who would work with the publishers. He also sent instructions for one of the first copies to be posted to the James Sisters in care of general delivery at Round Rock, Texas.

Two:

*The Countess
and the
Wonderful Shipboard Romance*

Rick took his leave of the sisters with great reluctance. Inexperienced as he was in the ways of love, he still knew he could have developed feelings for Shanda. The stirrings were there...but alas, there was no time.

Though he enjoyed their company, Rick determined it was time to experience travel on a genuine Mississippi riverboat. The Delta Queen was docked and soon to depart, so he made plans to board.

Some might see this as a diversion from his plans to go West, but Rick knew that such a venture meant more than catching a wagon train down one of the established trails leading from St. Louis. West meant any of the soil on the other side of the Mississippi river. The bright and beaconing star known as Texas also intrigued him. His plans would be flexible.

The atmosphere around the vessel reminded him of a county fair. People stood on the shore, waving to departing passengers. Stevedores shuffled and loaded last minute cargo. The air was pungent with animal smells, new leather, cotton bales, sacks of feed, and a variety of other items. It produced an exotic and memorable aroma. Rick recorded it in his journal.

After partaking in the waving and well-wishing necessary to separate those on shore from those making the trip, Rick headed for the bridge to see the captain.

The wheelhouse was over sixty feet above the surface of the water. It offered a wonderful view of the river and the surrounding countryside. The landscape passing slowly alongside was green and lush.

The sailor at the wheel looked over at Rick as he entered and said, "Passengers aren't allowed up here."

"Is the captain up here?"

"He's over there, on the deck," he indicated a tall man in a blue coat with gleaming brass buttons with a nod of his head. "He's talking to some other passengers."

Rick went down to meet him. "Captain McGuyver?"

"Aye, laddie, at your service."

Rick introduced himself and explained that he was a writer in search of material. He asked for permission to visit the wheelhouse, and for the privilege of interviewing him.

The captain was a short man, round, and had a fine flowing moustache and bushy sideburns. He seemed to wear a permanent look of barely subdued amusement. "And do you plan on using proper names in this book of yours?"

Rick shrugged. "It is up to the individual. I shall if you wish, or not, as you please."

The captain clasped a hand on his shoulder. "Well, my friend, I don't have a girl in every port as sailors are reputed to have, but I do have two ex-wives who would like to get their hooks into me. I don't think I need to assist them by advertising my present location in a book."

"I understand."

"No, lad, I don't think anyone who does not have two screeching harpies after his blood can fully understand, although I do thank you for your sympathy."

Having given up cigars, after finding them a bit harsh for his taste, and *so* big that he couldn't seem to hold them in his mouth in any manner he felt looked even halfway attractive, he gave the remaining ones to the captain. In their place, Rick acquired some much shorter, pencil-thin cigars. He found the smell much milder and they produced far less of the distasteful juice in his mouth, and Rick thought they were more in keeping with the thin features of his face. He still was not comfortable actually *lighting* them, but perhaps in time.

Rick strolled down the deck with his new Western hat at a slightly rakish angle. He found the effect produced exactly what he had in mind. He reaffirmed this conclusion with a reflection in a porthole. He was thinking on that, and on Shanda's eyes. Shanda had been very beautiful, and she certainly didn't rely on special trimmings to enhance her beauty. She didn't need to. And she did have the most remarkable eyes. Prior to meeting her, Rick had never thought brown eyes to be particularly outstanding, but hers were...well, they were...they were as amazing as those looking at him in the reflection now.

Rick turned to find the eyes regarding him over a black lace fan. They did not look away. Caught in their magnetic field, he went over. "Texas Jack Hammer," Rick said, "at your service." He swept off the big hat in a fairly creditable bow. "I seem compelled to come to your side."

"My name is Carmella," she responded with only a hint of a curtsy, fan still in place. She spoke with a hint of an accent that he couldn't place. "What part of Texas are you from?"

"Actually, I've never been there." Her eyebrows went up. "You see, I'm a writer, ma'am, and that's a pen name. Lots of writers use them."

"In the West, many people take new names, and sometimes on board ships."

Rick raised an eyebrow. "Are you saying Carmella is not your right name?" He looked at her frankly. "It's a Spanish sounding name, and you don't look to be of Spanish descent, although appearances can fool a person." Then Rick thought about what he was saying and hastened to add, "Oh, I'm sorry, I'm not thinking. Of course it is none of my business."

She smiled, "On a ship one should not use their right name, particularly if one anticipates having a shipboard romance."

"You are having such a romance?"

"You are very forthright, Mr. Texas Jack, are you not?"

"I suppose I am, please excuse me. It is an occupational hazard."

"I am working on such a venture, but he doesn't seem to be responding so far."

"Perhaps I can help. As a writer, words are my business."

"Then perhaps you will call on some of them to ask me to have a drink with you."

The realization hit Rick like a wet towel as it dawned on him who her target was. His collar was suddenly very tight, and he had to insert a finger in it to allow himself to swallow. When he accomplished an answer it seemed to him that his voice was high and thin. She appeared not to notice.

"It would be my very great pleasure." Rick offered his arm, and they strolled toward the main salon. Rick worked hard at retaining his composure, being inexperienced with the fairer sex. In the polite society where he came from, he had not yet progressed beyond the hand holding stage. It gave him a tingling sensation to be walking this fascinating creature into the salon.

Seated there, Rick ordered a couple of glasses of wine, another new experience, but one that seemed to be called for. The fan was down now, and he decided she was surely *not* Spanish. Her eyes were not as dark, as was common for Spanish *señoritas*, hazel to be exact. Her skin was very fair, and her hair was far too light. Still, her gown was very Spanish, and a deep violet in color. "What part of Spain are you from?" Rick asked.

The fan went back in place. "You are a writer. Who do you wish me to be, and where do you wish me to be from?"

A young lady looking for love? Rick could manufacture a shipboard romance story that he could definitely use. Still, he should be cautious, he didn't know why she played this game. He should guard his wallet for sure. To get a good story, though, Rick should play it to the hilt.

Aloud he said, "I would say Carmella is quite correct. And I think you are from Barcelona, from a very old and very grand family. I think maybe your grandfather was something of a rascal, perhaps a seafaring man, which accounts for your light coloring."

The fan fluttered, "How very perceptive you are."

Rick summoned the waiter. "In the light of this new information, I must apologize for putting this common fare in front of you." The waiter arrived and he said, "Waiter, please remove this domestic beverage, and return with some champagne, properly chilled, of course."

"Very good, sir." The waiter's eyes lit up at the prospect of his gratuity increasing.

Even though Rick was unaccustomed to drinking spirits, he knew young people drank wine from a very early age in other countries. He guessed this to be the case with the young lady. He resolved to carry through with his part. "You have been forced to flee from your country by the conflict there?"

She looked down. "It is very sad what is happening in my country."

"How you must have suffered."

"We must not think of it, we must think of only the present. It helps me put it from my mind."

"Of course."

They continued to have a wonderful conversation over drinks, then over dinner. It was full of mystery and intrigue. She was writing his tale for him. He, in return, had dashing and adventurous tales to recount for each of her heart-wrenching stories. They spent the entire evening in a make believe world of high adventure and excitement, fueled by the light-headed condition induced by the drinks.

The rising of the sun found them still in their places, enjoying the exchange. Yet, with the early rays of morning, the mood began to turn. A steward brought them coffee. They would dock soon.

She smiled, he thought a little sadly. "I've had a wonderful time. Although you know I haven't told you a word of truth all night."

"I've stretched the limits a bit myself, but then that's a writer's prerogative."

"I must tell you, I'm not from Spain. I live in Baton Rouge, in Louisiana. I've been away to school for a number of years. I'm on my way home to an almost certain marriage with one of a drove of well brought up but exceedingly dull young men who frequent our home when I am there. I wanted one wonderful adventure before I resigned myself to such a fate, and you have provided it in the grandest possible fashion, better than I could have ever imagined."

Rick blushed. "But, why me? There are much more handsome men on board, men who are experienced lovers. Men who would have given you an evening to remember."

"You gave me just such an evening. I wanted an adventure. I could sense you were pursuing one as well. You took me to a land more spectacular than mere realism could ever approach."

"And what an adventure. I'm afraid I don't want to part."

"Nor I, but we would be very disappointed in each other in the environment off the boat. Besides, you have many exciting things ahead of you yet. How I do envy your freedom to pursue your dream, and chase that magnificent star."

"I shall call it *The Countess and the Wonderful Shipboard Romance.*"

"What?"

"My book, I shall send a copy to Carmella De La Garza, general delivery in Baton Rouge. Check periodically for it and accept it as a token of my everlasting affection."

"That is very sweet. Be assured I will never forget our time together either, and I shall watch for all of your books."

With a tender kiss and a last meaningful look, they disappeared into the crowd at the New Orleans dock. She to her preset future, and he to catch a packet across the gulf to Galveston, Queen city of Texas, and his jumping off point into the West.

Trails of the Dime Novel

30

Three:

Pirates of Galveston

The moon leaked a ribbon of liquid silver in a stream leading toward me across the dark water...

Rick composed his latest masterpiece on a crate down on the dock at Galveston. A silk top hat was pushed back on his head, and he wore the finery, complete with waistcoat that was the standard uniform in the opera house, the first in Texas. He had just come from a performance there. It's true he hadn't kept his word about never wearing a tie again, but under the circumstances it was appropriate.

When the muse had come upon him, Rick had forfeited the remainder of the evening's entertainment to seek solitude so the words would come forth. He opened the journal and began:

Galveston is a spoiled brat of a city, living fast and wild, making her own rules as she goes. It used to be greatly feared as the dwelling place of the dreaded Karankawa Indians, avoided for their peculiar habit of eating people. Later, it was the hideout of the Pirate Jean Lafitte, scourge of the Caribbean, but savior of General Jackson at the Battle of New Orleans. A very complex man. It is said that pirates still abound in this magical place.

Rick was so caught up in this task that he barely noticed the old man sitting nearby, mending a net, until he said, "Mister, you shouldn't be down here on the docks dressed like that."

Rick looked up to acknowledge the old man for the first time. The man wore some sort of faded uniform and seaman's cap. His face was weather beaten, and his beard completely white. The old gentleman smoked a pipe, and in the still air the smoke hung about his head like a small cloud.

"Are you saying my attire is inappropriate?"

"Not if you're looking to get a free sea voyage, or your wallet lifted."

Rick went over to extend his hand. "I'm Rick Dayton, I write under the name of Texas Jack Hammer."

"Write? Write what?"

Rick pulled a copy of the dime novel that he had purchased at the hotel that very morning. It was the first he had ever seen with his name on it, so he had bought them all.

"It's entitled *The Daring Daylight Train Robbery*, and I confess I've been dying to show it to someone. Have you perchance read one?"

"I can't read, but it's a right pretty book."

"Would you like me to read it to you?"

"What a queer notion! But I'm gonna be here a good while getting these nets mended."

Rick pounced on a crate next to the man with enthusiasm. He fished out his glasses again. "I shall, then. I'd like to get your opinion on it."

He sat, opened the book with a flourish, and began to read. The old man pretended to scarcely listen, but Rick could tell he was interested.

He was barely underway when three men walked up on unsteady legs. They wore the unkempt clothes of ordinary seamen, and reeked of rum.

"'Ere now, what's this?" the largest of them, in a knit cap and striped shirt said. "Ere we be combing the streets for a fat purse, and not a penny to be found, and now providence up and sets one right at our doorstep."

Rick looked up at the man, turned over in his journal, and described him as 'swarthy'. His face brightened. "Ah, Captain Joe, it's just as you predicted."

Rick turned to look at the men. "What's it to be, gentlemen, impressment, or merely robbery?"

"This ain't right, Scudder," a little rat-faced man took his comrade by the arm to whisper to him in a voice that came across as more of a stage whisper.

"The fellow's daft."

"You're right about that," Captain Joe said, "he ain't got both his oars in the water. Boys, you oughta let him be."

Scudder said, "Hard pickins or easy, it's all the same to me. I'm not of a mind to miss a tidy return just because this bloke's clockworks are messed up."

"Clockworks?" Rick's puzzlement was clear on his face. "Oh, I see, you think I'm crazy."

The third man, a round-bellied seaman who went by the name of Chubb, dropped suddenly on the top of a crate as his legs seemed to fail him. He spoke for the first time. "He'd 'ave to be off his beam to be down 'ere inviting mayhem like this." He looked at Rick, leaning forward as though having to peer through a fuzzy haze. "And dressed like a swell?" He seemed to make up his mind. "Yup, the fellow's daft."

"Not at all, gentlemen, not at all. I'm merely gathering material for my next book. I'm a writer, my name is Texas Jack."

The rat-faced man said, "Hey, Scudder, I done heard of this galoot." He looked at Rick. "That book about the train robbery, you writ that?"

"I did."

"And you're gonna write us into one?"

"That depends on whether or not you do something interesting enough to write about."

Captain Joe paled. "Lord help, why don't you just hand them a Billy-club?"

The little fat man said, "Say, we could knock him in the head, and sell him to the master of the Star of the East Indies, he's looking for hands." He looked at Rick. "You could write about that!"

"Dear me, gentlemen, we don't have to go to so much trouble. We could instead repair to yon tavern, and I could buy refreshments while you tell me in great detail how you *might* have done it. The information is all I require, I don't have to actually undergo the experience."

Scudder looked confused. "That don't hardly seem right."

"I'd be happy to pay for your time."

"You'd stand the drinks, and pay us to talk on top of it all?"

"As long as my money holds out."

"Done!"

The three linked arms with Rick, and headed in a more or less straight line for a tavern called the Crow's Nest. Captain Joe followed in their wake, muttering, "This I got to see."

Safely seated in the tavern with pewter mugs of ale in front of them, Rick posed the question. "So, what would you have done?"

The greasy little man, Portugal by name, leaned forward and said, "Scudder there would have knocked you senseless with that sap in his pocket and we'da 'auled you off to the boat." He laughed a noiseless laugh, enjoying the vision he was picturing.

"It's too thin, gentlemen. You told me that much out on the dock. My readers require more action, more detail."

Chubb roused himself, "Say, what if you turned out to be a prize fighter, like that Sullivan feller. You could thrash us all soundly. Your readers would like that, wouldn't they?"

Scudder glowered. "I don't think I'd like that."

"It doesn't matter, I could never write it convincingly. I've never even seen a fight, much less participated in one."

Scudder pulled himself up to his full height. "Well, put your dukes up and I'll show you."

"I think not."

"Well...err...uh, let's see..." He walked over to the nearest sailor, and tapped him on the shoulder.

The man looked up and said, "What's up, mate?"

Scudder hit him full in the face, and the man went flying backwards, taking table and all with him. Drinks went showering. A companion said, "That be my drink, mate," and, coming out of his chair in a rush, put his full weight behind a punch that caught Scudder on the chin.

Portugal landed on the fellow's back, and with his free hand began clawing for the man's eyes. "Here now," the sailor bellowed, flinging the little man into the corner. He had no sooner divested himself of his burden than Chubb hit him a solid punch that dropped him like a sack of feed.

The entire room exploded into action. Men drained the last swallows of drink, then turned and hit the nearest target, often their best friends.

Rick huddled in the corner with Captain Joe, who said, "I hope you be happy, mate. This be a fine kettle of fish. We'll be lucky if we gets out with our skins."

Rick wrote as fast as his pencil would allow. "This is wonderful," he said as the words flowed.

The tavern erupted in fisticuffs. Blood splattered and chairs splintered as men struck and bit and clawed like savage animals. Shipmates fought among themselves as if they had never met one another. He paused to duck a flying bottle. *And standing in the middle of it all, the three gallant sailors stood back to back against all odds, defying those who would come against them...*

Looking over his shoulder, Captain Joe said, "You talking about those three idiots? You make them out to be heroes? They was set to cut your throat."

"Someone has to be the heroes. They're the only ones in this fight I know."

"Well, you do what you got to do, but if I be you, I'd clear this here port afore people get to figuring you be the one who started this mess."

Rick's head came up. "Ah yes, that would be

unfortunate. I take it you're leaving?"

"As fast as these old legs will get me out of here."

"I'm right behind you."

Four:

The Delicate Dilemma

The three bilge rats had a point. Sea experience was what Rick needed before he continued his exploration of the West. Still, an impressment gang was not the desired means of achieving it, as far as he was concerned.

Instead Rick struck an arrangement with Captain James Donovan, the owner and operator of the beautiful schooner *Utopia*. Donovan had been in the tavern the evening before when it was nearly destroyed by a brawl of magnificent proportions. Being seated at a nearby table, he had overheard how it had come about, to his intense amusement.

Rick met him at the Harbormasters office the following day. The good captain was perfect to play the hero in one of his adventures. Tall and handsome, he wore a simple uniform, but filled it out quite suitably. He had green eyes that could look straight through a man, and a very disarming smile that devastated the ladies.

Captain Donovan said he could not in good

conscience pay Rick to sail with him as he was inexperienced, and would be more of a liability than an asset for much of the trip. Since Rick willing to work and learn, however, he could hardly charge him as a regular passenger.

A compromise was struck. Rick would pay his way, but at a reduced rate. He would, in return, work on the vessel, with the understanding that he would still have sufficient time to pursue his writing.

Rick was introduced to the crew as Texas Jack, and they seemed to find the idea of having a writer on board intriguing, to say the least.

The vessel was consigned to carry goods to a British outpost in the East Indies, and return with trade goods destined for the Texas port of Galveston. Both instances suited his purposes admirably.

It went well, and a month into the voyage found the captain leading a party ashore on a small island in search of fresh water. They were far off the charted sea lanes, blown off course by a series of nasty squalls. The captain was unfamiliar with this island.

It was Rick's first encounter with a tropical island. He couldn't get over how blue the water was, and how absolutely crystal clear. The sand on the beach was white and pristine, and there were palm trees and greenery in evidence everywhere.

They were barely off the beach when they met a man. He had an unkempt beard, and his hair was long and stringy...he was half-naked...and he was white.

The man froze in his tracks, his mouth gaping. He half turned to run, then hesitated.

Donovan said, "Hold your peace, man, we mean you no harm."

Still poised for flight, the man's eyes darted from face to face like a scared animal. Finally he found a voice, "Who be ye?"

"I'm Captain James Donovan. That's my schooner off shore. Who is it I'm addressing?"

The confusion left the man's face as long observed discipline took over. He pulled himself straight as he answered. "I be Marlin McGregor, Seaman First, your worship, late of the *Texas Star* out of Galveston."

The man's uniform was in tatters. When he gave what passed for a smile, the gaps gave testimony to many missed dental appointments.

"And how do you come to be in this place, Seaman McGregor?"

"We ran aground in a storm, sir. Seven of us got away afore she broke up." He looked down and his voice got quiet. "The rest were caught below decks. It were some eight year ago, as I make it."

"Too bad. No way for good sailors to go." He paused a moment before adding, "You said seven?"

"Aye, sir, the first duty was to the passengers, and we had two. We were able to get them off, Reverend Otis Malone and his wife Rebecca. They be missionaries, sir, or they were."

Donovan waited him out.

"The rest of us what made it were the deck watch. The crew had been up all night fighting the storm and were getting a spot of rest when we hit the reef."

"And your captain?"

"Captain Kirk Donald, sir, and a finer man never lived. One of the crew looked in on him, but his cabin was awash, and he was nowhere to be seen."

Donovan nodded somberly. "Fitting, I suppose, that a captain would go down with his ship. But unfortunate, of course."

"Yes, sir. Anyways, I was at the wheel, and there were three Able Seamen on deck, Tolliver, Lebeau, and Jackson. Tony, the cabin boy, had just brought me a mug of coffee, so he was on deck as well." He smiled. "We plucked him out of the water after we hit."

"Well, Mr. McGregor, it sounds as if you acquitted yourself admirably. Let us go meet the others. Where would they be?"

"Native village, sir, there be a lot of them. Fine people by my say, and they took us right in."

"Very well, lead the way."

As they entered the village, they caused quite a stir among the natives. Some of the other survivors came out as well, the same unbelieving look on their faces that McGregor had shown. The first to recover was a giant of a man with fiery red hair and beard. In spite of the heat, he wore a string tie and a frock-tail coat. He grasped his lapels with both hands and announced,

"I'm Otis Malone."

Donovan was tall and muscular by ordinary standards, yet he was a head shorter than this man. The hand that engulfed his, as he answered, was huge.

"The missionary," Donovan said, returning the firm grip.

Malone shot a look at McGregor, who actually shrank from it physically. Donovan noticed the brief exchange.

Malone said, "I see Seaman McGregor has been running his mouth as usual. What'd he tell you?"

"Merely answered my questions. Where is your wife?"

Malone responded in a huffy voice. "My *former* wife is over tending the school. She is seldom anywhere else, if it's any of your business."

Donovan locked eyes with the man. "If you have any intention of shipping aboard my vessel, anything I choose to know about you is my business."

The look on Malone's face said he did not accept Donovan's statement, and he did *not* look away, but did not respond either. It was like an arm wrestling match contested with their eyes. It seemed to go on for a long time, though actually it lasted but a few seconds. Finally they looked away as if by mutual assent.

Donovan turned to his first mate. "Mister Sloan, will you be so good as to see to the fresh water? The cloud bank over yonder does not suit me, and this is not safe harbor."

"Aye aye, sir," the man said, turning on his heel to obey. He motioned for the rest of the shore party to follow him. "You heard the captain."

Donovan leaned over to Rick and whispered so the others couldn't hear. "Rick, I think you will want to stay with me. There may be a yarn in what we are about to encounter, though I would not have any mention of the possibility at this point."

Rick nodded, "I think you're right, Captain. I'll be as quiet as the ship's cat stalking a rodent stowaway."

Donovan turned his attention back to the survivors. "If you intend to go with us, you had better gather your belongings."

Malone said, "We barely got away with our lives, there's little else to gather."

"Very well, Reverend, just make ready if you're going."

"I no longer use that title."

Donovan raised an eyebrow.

Malone glared at him. "And that truly *is* none of your business."

Donovan's reply was cut short by a woman's voice behind him. "I won't be going with you, Captain, but I thank you for the offer."

Donovan spun, and took his cap off in the process. In front of him was a small, very beautiful blonde girl. He couldn't help but glance at Malone. She could be his daughter. A dozen questions obviously ran through his mind at once, but he held them in check. Instead he said, "Mrs. Malone, I presume." He gave a slight bow. "And this is Rick Dayton."

Mrs. Malone was dressed in a very colorful native sarong, festooned with a flower print. Living in the sun had made her almost as tan as the natives. She had eyes as blue as the lagoon.

She responded with as slight a curtsey, "Captain...Mr. Dayton."

Donovan replaced his cap. "Mrs. Malone, I could not in good conscience go off and leave you alone in such a place."

"Thank you for your concern, Captain, but I'm afraid the decision is not up to you."

Donovan thought on it a moment before he answered. "With all due respect, ma'am, I'm a little tired of people telling me what is and is not my business. Perhaps you people do not understand the nuances of maritime law. On the sea, a captain is judge and jury, president and governor. In the absence of any other authority I am it."

Malone's look was hostile, challenging, and the tone of his voice matched in kind. "That's only on your ship. You have no authority on this island. Actually here I..."

Donovan cut him off. "But you intend to come onto my ship, do you not?"

"Well, I..."

"There is something going on here, and I intend to get to the bottom of it before anyone sets one foot on my vessel. I do not intend to import trouble without a full understanding of what the difficulty might be, and a comfort level in my own mind that I may control it. Just so there is no misunderstanding, I am quite capable of sailing away and leaving the lot of you here exactly as I found you. Is this very clear?"

Had the proverbial pin dropped, it could have easily been heard over the stony silence that ensued. They did not like his words, but clearly recognized the truth in them.

There were some makeshift chairs nearby. Donovan took one of them. Malone and Rick settled in the others. Mrs. Malone excused herself and left.

Donovan said, "Malone, since you seem to resent it when anyone else offers explanations, and obviously consider yourself in charge here, I'll give you the first opportunity to tell me what I need to know to become comfortable with the situation."

Malone could not have communicated a more begrudging attitude if he had actually put it into words. He deposited his massive frame into a chair, and searched for what he must say.

"This is preposterous," he opened, "absolute blackmail."

"You don't have to do it. You and your little secret can simply remain on this island."

"Very well." It seemed to take a physical effort to squeeze out the words. "I was betrayed in a manner most evil and foul. A man of the cloth whose wife slept around like a common gutter snipe."

Donovan hummed a listening noise to urge him on.

"You see, she has a child, a colored little half cast. She didn't even have the decency to..."

Donovan gave the man time to compose himself. When he had, Malone drew himself up and said, "Damn you for making me do this. Well, I threw her out, naturally. I could do no less. It ruined what ministry I might have had with these people as well. I kept wondering which of them..."

Malone let out a heavy sigh. "And their women are no better. There are a dozen little half-breeds running around from one or more of this immoral crew of sailors. One sailor even considers himself married to one of these harlots, though there has been no formal ceremony. He had the unmitigated gall to ask *me* to..."

The ensuing silence prompted Donovan to say, "Is that it?"

"Isn't it enough? That slut humiliated me, ruined my ministry as well as my life, and if I could lay my hands on *him*!"

"I see. Very well, I shall want to talk to the others."

A storm cloud gathered on Malone's face. "You don't believe me?"

"I didn't say that. I'm a methodical man, *Mister* Malone. I gather facts before making a decision, and I never depend on a single source of information."

Donovan rose, and he and Rick made the short

walk to the little classroom. They walked in to find Mrs. Malone working with several children. Some were native, some obviously mixed race, and three who could easily pass for white. "Mrs. Malone, I came to get your side of it," Donovan said.

"Such formality on such a small island is ridiculous, Captain. Please call me Rebecca, or Becky if you would rather. However, since I have no intention of going with you, your threats and intimidation do not impress me in the least." Her reply was firm but not unfriendly.

Donovan smiled. "If you do not intend to sail with us, why would you care if I know what this is all about? Surely you don't intend to let your husband have the final say on this?"

"I care even less about what he thinks than about what you might think."

Donovan liked this girl. "Then help me understand for the sake of the crew who saved you from the wreck. Surely you have friends among them, and I was serious that nobody will be leaving with me unless I come to understand what's happening here."

"Very well, they don't deserve to be punished for this."

"Which implies that you think you do?"

"Yes. I transgressed, I admit it. There's no excuse for what I've done."

"I'm certainly not a Bible-thumper, Mrs. Malone, but doesn't the God you believe in practice forgiveness?"

"Yes, and I do believe my sins are forgiven, but it is less easy to forgive yourself, Captain Donovan."

"I see."

"In the meantime, I'm doing my penance, and serve God the only way I know how. I've reached a number of people here, particularly the children."

"How interesting. You say you're a sinner, but are ministering to the people and doing God's work. Your husband is incredibly pious, but refuses to do any of it."

"I suppose so. It's not my place to judge the actions of anyone else."

"Very well, I'm listening."

"My husband married me to help him in his work. His idea of marriage is..." She composed herself. "Well, let me say this, he came to me on a number of occasions interested in producing a son. When it became clear to him that it would not happen, he stopped. He said it was inappropriate behavior for a man of God. Just because he had no needs...I mean...I'm still a young woman..."

Donovan waved her comments aside, "There's no need for you to go on with that, I understand. You don't have to justify yourself to me."

She composed herself and straightened her apron. "I had no intention of doing so, but I do have a son, and cannot go away and leave him."

"Of course not, you must bring him with you."

"No, I can't, and I have said enough."

"If you're worried about how he would be accepted back home..."

"I'm not, but I have told you enough to clear the members of the crew from this mess, and I have given you all I intend to say."

Donovan left more puzzled than ever.

As soon as they were out of her hearing, Donovan looked at Rick and said, "The woman is hiding something, but what? She has said all she is going to say, but I'm not satisfied."

"I agree. Something is going on, but hanged if I know what it is."

They searched out McGregor, and found the man waiting anxiously by the launch on the beach. He had scant few possessions wrapped in a bandanna. He had given up the remnants of his uniform for the simple white pants worn by the natives. He appeared rather nervous.

The man looked up as they approached. "Find out what you need to know, Captain?"

"No, actually, I haven't."

McGregor's voice turned pleading. "Don't leave me on the beach, Captain, I give you my word I'm no part of what's going on here. I been nineteen year before the mast, sir, and I'd make you a hand, I would. I'd earn my keep."

"I believe you, Mister McGregor, and rest assured I'll not leave you behind, but I could use your help."

"Aye, sir, anything I can do."

"You can tell me what's going on."

"Aye, sir, that I will, what I know of it."

"I've talked to Malone and Rebecca. What they tell me doesn't add up."

"No, sir, that'd be like two people looking at the sky with one seeing blue sky and a few clouds, and the other seeing a bunch of clouds framed by a little blue. People can look at a thing and see it different ways."

"Are you a philosopher, Mr. McGregor?"

"Just an ordinary seaman, sir, but that doesn't mean I've given up my ability to think."

"Well put."

"What I see in this is a young lass, and treated like a bond servant, she was. I'd say she finally reached out for a little tenderness from the only place she could find it. I also see an old man whose concept of God is all rules and no compassion." He looked down and shook his head slowly. "Whatever be taking place, I can't find it in me to fault the lass."

"That pretty well sums it up for me as well, but why won't she leave and bring her son with her? She doesn't seem to fear the way he would be accepted back home."

"I don't know, sir. Maybe she doesn't wanna leave the work she's doing. She's a wonder, she is."

"Well, you've earned a ride, my friend. When the mate returns, tell him I said for you to help stow the provisions. And tell him I said to have you sign the articles. No reason you can't get paid for half a trip."

"Yes, sir! Thank you, sir!"

On the way back to the village, they met Able Seaman Jackson. His uniform was worn and faded, but clean and had been mended many times. He had long, shaggy blonde hair, and a heavy frame. The man looked down, scuffed the ground with his toe, and made an effort to work up enough nerve to speak. They stopped, and waited for the sailor to say what he needed to say.

"Beggin' your pardon, Captain, but might I have a word with ye?"

"It appears you are having a word with me, sailor."

"Guess I am at that, Gov'nor." He paused again, and when he composed himself the words came out in a torrent. "Captain, I have to take Leanna with me when we go. I'd work off our passage, for her and for the two kids. If it didn't cover it, I'd pay the difference, I swear I would." He went down to his knees. "Captain, you can't break up a family."

"Off your knees, man. I'd not split your family up."

There were tears in the seaman's eyes as he got up. "God bless you, sir! On the ship you'd marry us proper, wouldn't you, sir?"

"I would."

"So they can go?"

"Make them ready, Mr. Jackson, and get them out to the ship."

"Thank you, sir," then fading as he ran down the

trail, "thank you...thank you..."

"I should have asked him what he knew of all of this, Mr. Dayton." He smiled, "Perhaps later. His mind is occupied right now."

"I'd say that was an understatement, Captain."

Tolliver and Lebeau waited for them on the outskirts of the village. Tolliver was a hulking man, probably once very muscular, but it had gone to fat. He was balding, and to be honest looked a bit simple in the head. Lebeau, on the other hand, was as French as his name. He was a small man with a thin moustache and roguish good looks. It was Tolliver who spoke. "Are we set to go, Captain?"

"The price of passage is honesty, Mr. Tolliver. Are you prepared to pay the fare?"

"I got no secrets, sir."

"Nor do I," said Lebeau.

"Very well, gentlemen. You know by now what I am trying to learn. Tell me what you know, or think you know."

Tolliver continued as spokesman. "I know Malone ain't right in the head, and everybody on the island is affeared of him."

"Does that include you?"

"It does."

"Is that what's behind all of this, Malone's temper?"

"I reckon it'd be the biggest part of it."

Lebeau nodded his agreement, then added, "If not

all of it. If Malone could have found out the man who put the horns on him, he'd have killed him sure."

"Killed him? Surely not a man of the cloth."

"No doubt in my mind," Lebeau said.

"Nor mine," Tolliver agreed.

A mischievous glint came into Donovan's eyes. "You men know anything about these little light skinned kids running about?"

"*Mon ami*," Lebeau whined, "eight years is an eternity."

"I'm not passing judgment, it's merely a question. Are you going to want to take someone back with you?"

"You don't have enough room," Lebeau said.

"My wife wouldn't like it," Tolliver added, "that is, if I still got me a wife."

"I see, go down to the launch and prepare to ship out."

They ran toward the beach. As an afterthought, Tolliver stopped and saluted. "Yes, sir!"

Donovan turned and looked around the village. "Mister Dayton, I'd say that only leaves one."

"Yes sir, it does."

"The cabin boy, Tony Gallegos. I'm told he held that position eight years ago when their voyage began. I don't know if you are aware, but that position traditionally is something of an understudy role, leading hopefully to be a midshipman, and ultimately a ship's officer."

"I see."

They found the young man sitting alone on the edge of the village. His head was down, and he was dressed in simple native clothes. He was clean-shaven, and had light brown hair that fell to his collar. He was very tan and had an easy grace about him. He rose as they approached, and was obviously waiting for them.

"You'd be Tony?" Donovan asked.

"Yes, sir."

"Sit down, sit down," Donovan sat with him. Rick stood off to the side. "Have you gotten your stuff together?"

"There's no need. I'm not going."

"No?"

"There's no way I'll go off and leave Becky here alone."

Donovan's clear blue eyes surveyed the young man appraisingly. The look was returned, but it was a frank exchange, unlike the earlier hostile one with Malone. "I see."

"No, sir, you don't. Becky accepted all the blame for this, but it's time for it to stop."

"I take it you know something about this?"

"I know all of it. Since you are leaving, I guess it wouldn't hurt for you to know the whole story. It'd feel good to get it off my chest."

"Suppose you tell me, then."

"All right, I was seventeen when the ship wrecked. Becky was only eighteen. I hated the way he treated her, sir, I really did. To make a long story short, we became friends, really good friends. One night we took a swim together, and well, making no excuses the plain fact is, her baby is mine."

Donovan was skeptical. "A half cast? I'm sorry, Tony, but I don't believe that. A child of the two of you would most certainly be white."

"The baby you're thinking of isn't ours. The child everyone thinks is hers was born to a native girl on the other side of the island the preceding day."

"You switched babies because of Malone?"

"He would have killed both of us."

"Everyone seems to agree on that."

"So you see, she can't leave with her real baby, Malone would know and neither of us would survive the trip. Besides, she's also very attached to her adopted baby, as well. There is no choice but to stay here. We would like you to marry us before you leave, however. With Malone gone, it would finally be safe."

"I understand. Yes. Suppose you go get Becky and meet me at the ship. We'll see if we can't set this situation right."

By the time Donovan made the trip to the *Utopia*, he had Seaman Lebeau and Rick in tow.

The couple waited. Becky looked nervously at them, but Donovan reassured her. "Don't worry, they know all about it. Mr. Lebeau and Mr. Dayton will serve as a witnesses for your wedding."

She appeared to relax.

"But we also have a little proposition to put before

you."

The young couple clasped hands, and looked at him anxiously.

"First, we're prepared to do the marriage just as you want. The resulting problem will be that you won't be legally divorced, so..."

Tears formed in the corners of her eyes. "We've thought about that. It's a terribly sinful thing, as all of this is, but as long as we stay on this island, we think we can live with it."

"I'm afraid I don't agree. I'm sadly fear it would work on you. I'm not sure you could ever come to terms with it, particularly given your religious convictions."

The wetness in her eyes turned to streams. Tony covered both her hands with his own and said, "We have no other choice."

"Perhaps I can offer you one. Lebeau has agreed for me to tell Malone that I married him and, what's the name of the native girl you exchanged children with?"

"Shaniella."

"Right. Shaniella's excited about the chance to go to the New World. You've apparently told her a lot about what it's like. At any rate, this way you get to take both kids, right under his nose, with him none the wiser. When you are able to get back, and get a legal divorce, you can set this situation right."

"Will it work?" Tony asked.

"Of course it'll work."

She looked at Lebeau. "Why would you do this?"

"It is simple. *Le amore*, a Frenchman is always ready to advance the cause of love."

She came over to hug his neck.

"Besides," he continued, "Shaniella is lovely, no? Who knows, by the time we finish our journey...we may find the time for pretending is over."

"Yes," Becky said, "isn't it wonderful? The time for pretending will be over."

Rick couldn't write the story. Even changing the name of the young people, their identity could not be disguised.

The voyage itself was very tenuous at first due to the irascible Mr. Malone, but some strange quirk of providence saw him washed overboard during a squall on the dogwatch the second day out. Those who had the deck watch were saddened to report that they were unable to do anything to help him. He was simply there one minute and gone the next. If Donovan had any concerns about these sailors and their relationship to Malone, he kept it to himself. He genuinely hoped the man really did wash over the side.

This event prompted the young couple to share their strange tale with the ship's company. The wedding immediately followed and a substantial party ensued. Donovan turned his cabin over to the couple as a honeymoon suite, saying, "I guess it's true, God really does work in mysterious ways."

This freed Rick to tell the tale. He titled it *The Delicate Dilemma*. It began"

It was a beautiful tropical island, calm and serene. Little did the sailors know it hid a deep and dark secret...

Five:

The Ride

The *Utopia* made port in Galveston. Early the following morning, Rick made his way down to the barbershop in the lobby of the beachfront hotel. The aroma that overpowered him as he entered took him back in time.

Rick had loved barbershops ever since he was a youth. *Well, all right, so I'm not exactly an old man, but these experiences I've been having are aging me fast.*

When the smell of that hair tonic hit him, he was five years old again, sitting on that booster seat, getting a hair cut. It could easily have been the very same establishment. The shaving cups lined up in the case, the mirrors on the wall facing each other so your image is repeated over and over going off into infinity. The *thap-thap-thap* of the shoe shine at the end of the room. It was a place for real men.

Rick sat down, drawing in a deep breath and holding it, savoring it. Then he noticed the man next to him was reading one of his books, *The Pirates of*

New Orleans.

The man glanced up and smiled at Rick, then returned to his reading, chuckling now and then. He was a prosperous looking man, dressed in a simple but well cut suit. He had a substantial girth, but carried it well. Obviously a man who liked to eat well, but who exercised to work it off.

Rick enjoyed his reaction to his writing. Suddenly he paused as if he had just had a revelation. The man turned to the back of the book, looked at Rick's picture, then gazed curiously at Rick. "I don't mean to be rude, but are you..."

"Not rude at all. Yes, I am Rick Dayton. I write under the name of Texas Jack Hammer."

"Well, I'll be. I wouldn't expect...I mean, you look so young...aw, dang it, what I mean is..."

Rick held up a hand. "It's all right. I'm quite accustomed to people expecting me to be much older."

"Well, this is quite an honor." He extended a hand. "I'm really enjoying your little tale here. These here fellows are something else."

"You should have met them in person."

"You mean they're real?"

"I could hardly do them justice, they were such colorful characters."

"I admit I figured you to just be making this stuff up."

"Not at all. It requires a lot of research to write this material, experiences, interviews, a feel for the location."

"Where you headed now?"

"In search of my next tale. I don't really plan them. I find fate provides ample opportunities."

"Maybe it's fate that put us here together. How would you like to come stay at my ranch, and soak up a little of that atmosphere you're looking for?"

"That's very kind of you. I'd be delighted."

"You could stay at the main house. My wife would love it."

"If it wouldn't offend you, I'd rather stay with the men in the bunkhouse, and I'd like to try my hand at ranch work, to get the feel of it."

"I can't imagine working when you don't have to, but if you say so, it's all right with me."

It was only a three-day ride to get there. The cowboys took to Rick right off. They knew he was a dude, but the novelty of a writer in the bunkhouse interested them, as it had done the crew on the ship. In the evenings, Rick would read them a little from one of his books, and they'd reciprocate with yarns that gave Rick writers cramp just trying to keep up. And such yarns, Rick knew; they were inspired by the possibility of being captured in writing.

He captured the inventive stories in his journal for use when he began his tale:

Out here men are only first names. Choctaw is a

half-breed, Navajo and Irish, but I already know it's a major no-no to refer to anyone as a half-breed. It's considered very demeaning and quite likely to produce a fight. He moves with the stealth of a cat even without thinking of it, and his hair is a black so dark it shines. The tales he likes to tell are of the days of his youth, and he likes to tease the 'white eyes' about his underlying savage nature.

Hank is plain as a board fence and just as lanky. An Alabama boy, he served in the Civil War and has spine tingling stories about riding with Stonewall Jackson.

Fargo was born in the saddle and seems to have worked on a ranch his entire life. He's the oldest, so hard and weathered that his age is impossible to guess. I say not as old as he appears, though.

Rick got to know them a little better as he went along with them on a little trip to pick up some stock from neighboring ranches. The cowboys began talking about him around the fire after he got to sleep. At least, they thought he was asleep. He didn't let on that he could hear.

Fargo said, "I guess old Rick's all right, but he's sure got a lot to learn."

Hank smiled. "Yeah, every green hand's got to go through a little rawhiding, we all did."

"Usually we put them up on the worst horse in the remuda," Fargo looked thoughtful, "only we ain't got one with us."

Choctaw said, "We'll be at the LX tomorrow, they're working out a rough string."

Fargo's face brightened up. "How about it, boys, reckon he oughta pay his dues?"

The major nodded slightly, "I wouldn't expect him to be treated any different than anybody else as long as you remember he's new to all this, all right?"

"Sure thing, boss," Fargo said, turning to smile at the other hands.

The major assigned Rick to go out and help hold the herd while they branded the new stock. Then he rode off a short distance, but stayed where he could ease back quietly.

Fargo said, "There's no point in going clear out to the remuda." He looked at the foreman of the LX. "I'll bet you'd let him borrow one of your horses, wouldn't you?"

The men all grinned like possums in the moonlight as he said yes. Rick still didn't let on that he had heard their plans. He knew he had it to do.

A cowboy led one out. "He can use old Sunflower here." They began to throw a saddle on him.

Rick was scared stiff. Any horse worth his salt would pitch a little first thing in the morning, but they didn't have to be held by the ears until the rider got on. Even if Rick hadn't known their plans, this treatment would have been a dead giveaway.

He got on board and got a good grip on the saddle horn with his left hand. He gripped with his knees, took the reins in his right hand and said, "Okay, old fellow, let's go to work."

The horse pitched a couple of times, but not too badly. He just kind of humped his back a little, then fired out with his hind legs as if his heart really wasn't in it. Rick began to think he had misunderstood the intentions of the cowboys. As the hopping diminished, he even began to relax a little. Sunflower felt him ease up on the pressure of his knees. It was what the horse had been waiting for.

Sunflower suddenly went right straight up, and came down stiff legged, which jarred Rick to the bone. He immediately went straight up again, and somehow, on the way up, changed direction, and rolled to the right. He left Rick sitting in mid air.

Rick hit the ground like a sack of flour. It took a couple of minutes to clear out the cobwebs from his head. Laughing cowboys helped him up. The group on the corral fence was breaking up. The show was over.

Choctaw said, "You did all right. Now let's go get you a real horse and we'll go to work."

"I don't need another horse, I'm not through with this one yet."

"It ain't necessary, man. You've done what was expected of you. Let's go get to work."

Rick pulled his hat down tight. "Get a grip on him where I can get back up."

They dropped a rope on the horse, eared him down, and Rick climbed back on top. Cowboys began to drift back to the fence rail. The major rode in closer.

This time there was no warm-up. As soon as they released his ears, Sunflower went into a spin, going faster and faster until Rick could hold on no longer. He went clear out of the corral over the top rail, taking several cowboys with him. All of them watched in amazement as he climbed back over the fence and said, "Grab him!"

Rick stopped in front of the horse to look him full in the face. "Okay, I've seen that trick, what else you got?"

There was no argument now as they pulled the horse down and Rick mounted. This time it was a whole series of stiff-legged hops, followed by several tight turns with a couple of sunfishes thrown in. Then Sunflower did a massive leap and rolled over in the air. Rick came flying off.

The cowboys ran over, congratulating him on a great ride. One of them began to lead the horse back to the barn, but Rick said, "Where you going with that horse? We're not through with each other yet."

The cowboys all tried to talk him out of it. Then the major rode over, told them to knock off all the foolishness, and get back to work.

Rick said, "If you make it an order, then I'll do it, but if you aren't, then I'm not through; not by a long shot."

The major looked at him. He saw the set of Rick's jaw and the determination in his eye. "I understand. I'd never do that to you."

The ranch had come to a complete stop. Everyone was over there watching. Rick was thrown four more times in rapid succession...five...six...the cowboys began yelling and waving their hats, encouraging him. They started to rope the horse for him again, but Rick waved them off. "I don't want any more help. He knows it's between us now."

Rick put his foot in the stirrup and pulled Sunflower's head close with his left hand as he swung on board. The horse could do nothing but go in a tight circle with no power until his head was released, but then he went absolutely crazy. He did things horses simply can't do, and he threw Rick further than anyone could ever remember seeing someone thrown before.

Rick limped badly as he came back in. One eye began to swell shut.

Choctaw said, "Why don't you let me have a turn at him while you rest up?" Several other cowboys joined in asking for the same chance.

"Thanks," Rick said, "I know you guys want to try to wear him down where I can finish him off, but if you're any kind of friends you won't do that to me."

He limped up in front of Sunflower, who stood with his head down. It told on him, too, but as Rick reached out for the reins, the horse's head came up. This was a proud horse. They stood there and looked at each other for what seemed like a long time. Then Rick rubbed the horse's neck.

"You're a lot of horse, but unless you cripple me up, I'm going to be out here all day and all night until one of us breaks."

Rick was thrown eight more times, but each time he stayed on longer and longer. Sunflower started standing still to let him mount without any tricks. Then, as suddenly as it had started, Sunflower began responding to the rein. He went left, he went right, he stopped, then stood there with his head high, no less proud. The cowboys went crazy; they mobbed Rick and carried him off on their shoulders.

As they sat him down, Fargo held out his hand and said, "I don't reckon anybody will ever call you tenderfoot anymore."

Rick beamed.

The major rode from where he had watched into the middle of the little group. Choctaw said, "Boss man, I'd say you got yourself another top hand."

"I'd say so, too!" He smiled at Rick, then looked around. "We gonna do any work today, or are just have us a rodeo?"

The next day they lined out the herd to go to the next ranch. The group looked up to see the owner of the LX Ranch riding toward them. He had Sunflower on a lead rope.

The major said, "Good morning, Bill. What are

you doing out this way so early?"

"Satisfying my curiosity." He pushed his hat back on his head and crossed his hands on his saddle horn. "You know, four different ranch hands forked this knothead horse this morning, and he stacked all four of them up on the fence like cord wood. They looked like laundry hung out to dry. I thought Rick broke him yesterday, but it looks like he only tired him out. Of course, there is one other possible explanation."

"What's that?" The Major was curious.

There was a crowd now as the hands rode over to see what was going on. The rancher looked up and his eyes sought and found Rick. "Step down there, Texas Jack, I want to test out my theory."

Rick stepped down, and the rancher turned the horse loose. Sunflower came straight over and nuzzled Rick.

"That's what I thought," the rancher said. "Let's see you mount him."

Rick hurt in places he didn't even know he had, and fighting this horse again was the last thing in the world he wanted to do. He sighed, pulled the horse's head in tight with his left hand as had had started doing yesterday towards the end of the contest. The horse turned in a couple of tight little circles, then pitched as Rick let go of his head, but this time his heart really wasn't in it. After hopping around for a couple of minutes, he settled down and started answering the reins like a livery horse.

"Yeah, I thought so," said the rancher. "He's a one man horse now. He's yours, my friend. Sure no use to anyone else. You can tie him to a hitching rail most anywhere, because you can bet your boots nobody's gonna be stealing him."

"Thank you, sir, but I'd rather pay you for him."

"You paid me yesterday, it had to be the dad-blamedest battle I ever saw. I don't know when I've enjoyed anything as much. You just treat him right, and you'll never have a more loyal friend. Only, was I you, I'd give him a different name."

Rick thought for a minute and decided. "Yes, sir, I think you're right, and I know exactly what to call him."

"What's that?"

"I'm going to call him Sundown, sir, 'cause that's what I thought it would be before he gave up."

Six:

The Lucky Bed

Fredericksburg was a quaint little German community in the hill country of Texas, a perfect place for Rick to spend a pleasant weekend. For accommodations he ended up at a small stone walled roadhouse located in the heart of town.

Rick entered the house to step into a cozy living room. The fireplace facing the couch was the focal point of the room. But his attention was immediately drawn to the adjoining bedroom, and to the big, comfortable looking brass bed with what appeared to be a very, very old headboard. "They say it's lucky," Carter said. She was the innkeeper, a carefully but simply dressed woman in her early fifties. She seemed to be a no-nonsense lady from the ground up.

He was skeptical. "How can a bed be lucky?"

"How can anything be lucky? It just happens."

"What makes you think it's true?"

"Let me go into the kitchen, get us some refreshments, and I'll tell you."

She returned with some lemonade, then

continued. "The original owners, R.J. and Carolyn McKenzie, bought the bed back in the early 1800s. To put it in the vernacular of the period, they were dirt-poor farmers, barely squeaking by. For someone in those circumstances, such a bed as this was an incredibly lavish purchase. It was a spur of the moment thing, of course. They had some crop money in their pocket, and there it was. It probably cost as much as the sum total of everything else they owned, but they had to have it."

Rick said, "It sounds foolish to me."

"As it did to them. All the way back with it in the rear of their wagon, they couldn't believe they had done it, but they believed it that night when they got the best rest they had enjoyed in years, and they believed it nine months later when Leah was born."

"That doesn't sound lucky, considering their circumstances."

"It probably wouldn't have been, except their luck did change. They had a couple of very good years crops, put the money from them back into improvements, and started building their little farm into a very solid business proposition."

"Are you saying the bed caused it all?"

"I'm not saying anything, I'm only telling you a story, and you can draw your own conclusions."

Rick looked surprised, "You mean there's more?"

"Much more. I can tell you this, the McKenzies thought the bed was lucky, which is why they gave it to her younger sister, Diane, who was getting married. The object of the young lady's affection was Jack Wilson, a clerk at the dry goods store. Jack was an amiable young man, but hardly a spectacular catch as he made little money and had no ambition. The young couple was told how lucky the bed was, and true or not, they believed it. Sleeping in the bed made Jack a new man. Within a very short period of time, they had a baby on the way, and Jack's newfound confidence took him to the bank and an escalating role there, as well. They were believers, and the reputation of the bed was well on the way."

"I don't believe the bed had anything to do with it," Rick said. "He merely needed something to give him a push. It was more likely the added responsibilities of a new family."

"It could very well be. Still, when the couple could afford to move out of their little rent house and into better quarters they left all their furniture, including the bed, where it was because some struggling young people from the church they attended were coming into the house and had virtually nothing. They told the young people, Charles and Sandy Jackson, about the luck of the bed, and the couple said it was already lucky for them because of the good fortune it brought in the form of receiving the furniture. However, the young couple went on to establish a small repair business in the community which subsequently thrived."

"Coincidence."

"Very probably, but they believed otherwise, as did the original owners. You remember me mentioning R.J. and Carolyn McKenzie?"

"Yes."

"When their daughter Leah became engaged to be married, nothing would do but for her to have the lucky bed. They came and purchased it from the Jacksons, and gave it to Leah and her intended, Robert Green, as a wedding present. Robert had been struggling with a little ranch for some time. He made it clear he didn't believe in such a thing as a lucky bed, but it was very comfortable, and he was pleased to get it for its face value. Still, things did begin to improve at his place, and there seemed to be no tangible reason for it. I don't know he ever came to believe in the luck of the bed, but Leah did, and they did have a great deal of good fortune come their way."

Rick was unconvinced, but very interested.

Carter went into the next room and came back with a very old journal. "The reason I'm able to tell you these stories in such detail is because Leah started this diary of the bed, going back to the previous owners. The diary has been passed on with it through the years, with various owners telling tales of what they believe the bed has done for them."

She opened the book and began to leaf through the pages. "Following Leah was a dentist who came into a rather substantial inheritance shortly after acquiring the bed. Then a lady got it, and credited the bed with her missing in action husband in the Civil War turning up safe and sound."

She continued to turn pages. "It goes on and on down through the years, a barren older wife suddenly conceiving, happy families, illnesses cured. This house was built shortly after Mr. Weidenfeller arrived here from Germany with his infant sons. His wife died either shortly before leaving or on the journey. The bed proved lucky again as he courted and wed a Miss Metzger, and went on to have quite a good life here in Fredericksburg. All in all the diary is quite a remarkable record."

"When did it end?"

"It hasn't, when guests stay in that particular room, we ask them to write us if any feel they have had good luck following their stay. We've had many letters. It really is most gratifying."

"It's all in their mind."

"Perhaps it is, but what's wrong with that?"

"Well, I for one don't believe in it, but it's a clever little story to tell if you don't mind me using it. You see, I'm a writer. I write under the name of Texas Jack Hammer. Perhaps you've heard of me?

"No, I'm sorry."

"No matter, it's a pleasant little tale I shall call *The Lucky Bed*. And of course, it couldn't hurt to spend the night in it."

"Of course, what can it hurt? Can I help with your luggage?"

"I've got it."

When Rick returned with his bag, he found Carter standing inside the door, reading a letter. She had some other mail tucked under her arm. She smiled, then looked up to see Rick standing there. She said, "Isn't this nice, it seems a very pleasant gentleman who stayed with us a couple of weeks ago has broken the bank at a casino in Galveston." She looked at me. "Won't this look nice in my book."

Rick smiled. "It'll look even better in mine."

Seven:

The Battle of Adobe Walls

Rick absorbed the atmosphere around him. A genuine Western saloon was a new experience. He wrote his impressions into his journal:

Where I come from back East, a bar or lounge is generally where people go for a drink, or to be alone. Alone with their thoughts, or alone with someone they want to talk to. Perhaps a quiet drink after work.

Here in the West it's not a bar, but a saloon, and it is something quite different. It's a meeting place. Everyone for miles around ends up here, and shares information about who they've seen and where they've been. There are people here that don't even drink. I'm told on Sunday the place is cleaned out and church services are held here since there isn't a formal church in town yet. When it's used as the courtroom, the bar is closed while it's in session.

It's a recreation facility with a pool table and card games, and dancing to the rinky-tink piano. Not to mention what sort of recreational activity might be going on upstairs. There's a floor show and stage entertainment, and occasionally a good brawl.

Rick looked up from his notes, not really thinking that he was speaking aloud. "Quite an extraordinary place."

"Watcha writin'?"

Rick looked over his shoulder to find an old man in a buckskin outfit. He had an indistinguishably colored hat with the brim turned up flat in the front. His whiskers were salt and pepper gray, and the gaps in his teeth accentuated his unusual accent. He seemed to blur his words as much as his vision seemed to be. Actually, the man looked blurred himself, although Rick thought that could hardly be possible.

"Actually, I'm writing information to be used in a book. And whom might you be?"

"Whom?"

A man standing next to him said, "That's city talk fer who are you, Clem."

"Ohh, well I be Cactus Clem McFerson. Clem to my friends, or to anybody else, I reckon."

"And you?" Rick turned his gaze to the other man.

"Gopher Gus Tolliver."

"Please sit down, gentlemen, I'd like to stand you to a drink. Does everyone out here have such colorful nicknames added on to their names?"

"A lot do," Clem said as he lowered himself into a chair. "The nicknames are more important than the proper handle, generally."

"And why would that be?"

Gus stopped in mid-pout, looking over the top of the bottle. "Well, put it this way, there be a lot of Smiths out this way."

"You saying people don't use their right name?"

"We tend to judge folks more on what they is rather than what they was," Clem mumbled around his glass.

Gus said, "You ain't said who you be."

"I'm sorry, my name is Rick Dayton."

"Feller while ago called you Texas Jack," Clem said.

"Yeah," Gus added, "and here you be fussing about people what don't use their right name?"

"It's a pen name. I write under it."

"Mine's a pen name, too," Clem agreed, "after I shot a fellow I took to using it to keep from going to the pen."

Gus said, "Whatcha write in this book of yours?"

"Stories. I use whatever I find."

Clem twirled the end of his mustache. "I was at

the battle of Adobe Walls, I can tell you about that."

Gus snorted. "You was not! If everybody was there who claimed to be, woulda been six or seven hundred people there. Know fer a fact it was just thirty or forty."

"You don't have to tell me how many people was there, I was one of 'em." Clem was indignant. "Weren't many there when it started, but there was a right smart number by the time it was over."

Rick cut in. He didn't care whether the man was really where he claimed or not, if it was a good story. "Tell me about it."

Gus stomped off, muttering to himself. Clem took a long drink, stared off into space, and began his tale.

"You see, son, when I up and left home I went over to be with some kinfolks down in Coleman County, over in Texas. They had a ranch down there, and I signed on as a green hand. I made a bunch of trips up and down the Chisholm Trail with them.

"We had us a few scrapes on them drives, but nuthin' real serious. I got a mite tired of it, though, and reckon I wanted to do something different. Or maybe it was just the grass being a little greener over on the other side of the fence, but I heard about all the money to be made hunting buffaloes, so I took my horses, and pulled my stakes.

"The main outfittin' place along there was Jacksboro, so that's where I went. When I got there, I run acrosst ol' John Carter. Now John, he had him some wagons and was figuring on going hunting them critters. Reckon I proved up I could handle an ox-team, so he signed me on, and we pulled out. We headed over toward Guide Mound over on Wichita River. We crossed at Eagle Nest Crossing.

"We went up on the plains and gotta lotta hides. We was organized pretty good. We had shooters, and skinners, and peggers, an' of course wagon drivers. The shooters would follow the herd and shoot as many as they could, then the skinners would come along and peel th' hides off. The peggers would follow after that and stretch 'em out to dry. Finally, the wagons would come pick 'em up.

Rick said, "That seems pretty wasteful to me."

"Kinda looks that way now, but then it seemed like there weren't no end to them critters, and nobody thought nuthin' about it. Anyway, weren't long 'fore I graduated from a bullwhacker to a shooter. You see, I'm a good shot, and it was a whole lot less work."

He took a long pull on his drink. "Then one day we began to run outta supplies, and I went with Old Man Carter went over to Adobe Walls, where there was an outfittin' place rigged up. They had a saloon where ya could buy rotgut liquor, and a store where ya could buy ammunition and chuck and stuff. We spent the night by the fire. The next morning, one of the men was out hitchin' up his team when he come to notice something off in the distance, but he couldn't make it out. But as they fetched up closer, he seen it was a big bunch of

Injuns.

"He hollered and we run in and forted up, but there was two guys sleeping under their wagon that never had a chance.

"It was a pretty good little fight. Them Injuns would run up to th' door and try to knock it in. Then they'd back their horses up an' try to make them kick it in, but it weren't no good. All the while they'd be riding around them cabins whooping and a-shootin'. There was 'bout twenty-five, thirty white men in them cabins. Them Injuns mostly had bows and arrows, though a few of 'em had guns. They'd ride by hanging off the side of them horses and they'd shoot under the neck. They didn't reckon on them old Spencer rifles, though. They'd shoot right through a horse!"

Rick wrote as fast as he could. He looked up. "So, don't stop now...what happened?"

"Funny thing about them varmints. When things ain't going right they ride off a ways and make medicine. They whoop and holler and get all lathered up for a big charge. And that's what they did. They was way over on this hill getting fixed up to roll right over us, but I had me this old Sharps fifty caliber buffalo gun..."

"Aw that's it," Gus whined. "I ain't listening to any more of this hogwash." Gus had returned with a beer in his hand and a scowl on his face.

"Gus?" Rick said. "I didn't think you were listening."

"I was trying almighty hard not to, but this lying polecat is about to tell you about this famous shot he made." He got right in Clem's face "Ain'tcha? *Aint'cha*?"

Clem got a shadow of a smile on his face. "Well..."

"I told you this sidewinder was nowhere near that fight. Everybody knows it was Billy Dixon what run them Indians off that day."

"How could he have done that?"

"Guess I can't fault the story he told none, except the part about him being in it. Them scudders had backed off a ways to get themselves worked up to charge again, but Billy took his buffalo gun and walked outside. He drew him a bead on the Indian wearing the biggest, fanciest headdress and pulled the trigger.

"They stood there for several seconds, then all of a sudden that ol' chief just pitched off the back of his horse and lay there. The rest of them looked at how far it was back to the cabins, decided their medicine was bad, and rode off."

"How far was it?"

"An army surveyor measured it at over fifteen hundred yards."

"You're kidding!"

"Nope, ask anybody in the room. Whale of a shot, and this outlaw was fixin' to take credit fer it."

"Aw don't git yore bowels in an uproar. He was just looking for a yarn and I was spinning him one."

"In the writing trade we call that taking artistic

license."

Gus snorted. "Out this way we call it lying."

"Doesn't matter, gentlemen, it is indeed a heroic story. I shall call it *The Magnificent Shot*."

Eight:

Blazing Guns in Diablo

It wasn't much of a town. Half a dozen board buildings, a couple of tents, and several hitching posts, one of which Rick used to tie his horse. There were no discernible signs except for a faded *Saloon* over a weathered blue building down the street.

Seeking direction, he looked about and his eyes came to rest on a dapper gentleman standing in the middle of the dirt street. The man wore a dark blue suit, colorful vest, and had a gold watch chain hanging from his vest pocket. A pencil thin cigar jutted beneath the man's thin mustache, and narrowed eyes darted toward Rick as he approached him.

"Good day, sir, I wonder if..."

The stranger interrupted. "I don't mean to be rude, mister, but I'm a little busy here."

"Busy? But you are only standing in the middle of the street."

The stranger gave him a small smile. "I have some business to transact with the gentleman at the other end of the street."

"I'm sorry, I won't keep you then. I was merely seeking directions to the bank."

"The closest thing we have to a bank is the Wells Fargo stage office. That would be the red building over there."

"Thank you sir. I am in your debt. Perhaps I'll repay you by buying you a beverage after you complete your business."

"If I'm around when I complete my business, I'll take you up on that offer. Now you had best move out of the line of fire."

Rick walked toward the Wells Fargo office. "Line of fire?"

As he approached the office, a voice came from the inside: "You best get in here before you get your head blown off."

He stepped up on the porch. "I beg your pardon?"

"Can't you see those two are about to shoot it out? Have you lost your mind walking out between Ace Deadmon and Black Jack Wilson just as they're about to start slinging lead?"

"Slinging lead? What a wonderful expression! Can I use it?" Then, after a moment..."You mean they propose to have a gun battle?"

"Would you get off the porch and get in here?"

"But...but...I need to see this. It would make an excellent book."

"You can see all you need to see from in here." A hand reached through the door and pulled him inside the station. The hand was attached to an older gentleman, maybe in his sixties, with a white moustache and a perpetually worried expression. For his age his strength was surprising.

"I say, there's no need to get physical about it." Rick straightened his coat and extended his hand. "I'm Rick Dayton. I'm a writer."

"Jack Powell. I'm the station manager. Can we talk in a minute, I want to see this."

Rick pulled out his journal pocket and moved to the window. He noticed for the first time the heavyset man at the other end of the street. Dressed all in black with no coat, he had what appeared to be a two-day growth of beard, and even at this distance Rick could tell he had ugly and uneven teeth.

The two men had closed the distance to maybe thirty paces and were saying something to each other. They were too far away to hear the words.

"What are they doing?" Rick asked.

"Exchanging insults, most likely."

All at once both men reached for the pistols on their hips. Three shots sounded almost as one and the man called Black Jack spun and fell facing the opposite direction. His gun had not cleared the holster.

"My goodness, that was sudden!" Rick exhaled the breath he didn't know he was holding.

"Yeah, that Ace is fast."

"But it was over so quickly...somehow I expected more."

"They weren't out there to play games, fellow." Powell moved around behind the counter. "Did you say you were a writer?"

"Yes. I write under the name of Texas Jack Hammer."

"No kidding? Say, I got one of your books right over here. I believe it's called *The Countess and the Wonderful Shipboard Romance*."

"Ah, yes, one of my personal favorites."

"Did you actually do that stuff?"

"It would be most unseemly for a gentleman to say, but yes, there is a modicum of truth involved in the tale."

"Well, I'll be hornswoggled. Could I get you to sign this book?"

"I should be delighted." Rick wrote a brief sentiment and signed his name with a flourish, glancing up into the street as he did. Two men picked up the body of Black Jack and carried him toward the livery stable. The man called Ace made his way back to the saloon.

Rick said, "I don't believe this Black Jack person fired his weapon, did he?"

"Nah. I didn't figure him to have much of a chance against Ace."

"If he was so badly outclassed, why did he challenge this Ace person?"

"Most of the time it's some young guy who thinks he can get the job done. They usually can't."

"So they weren't evenly matched?"

"Mister, the really fast gunslingers never go up against each other. Not in an open fight, anyway."

"No?"

"No. You see, if they're that closely matched then they're gonna be firing at the same time, and odds are both of them will catch lead. Nobody wants to go into a fight where they are likely to die, win, or lose. Nobody but these young wannabes, anyway."

"I see. It's most unfortunate."

"Yeah. Was there something you wanted?"

"Yes, I need to send a telegram to my attorneys and replenish my supply of ready funds."

"I can take care of that for you."

They quickly transacted their business. Then Powell said, "You gonna write a book about this?"

"Of course. I think I shall call it *Blazing Guns in*...what did you say the name of this town was?"

"Diablo."

"*Blazing Guns in Diablo*, then."

"Well, I'll be. Will I be mentioned in it?"

"Do you wish to be?"

"Sure."

"Then you shall. I will also need to go over shortly and see whether this Mr. Ace wishes his real name to be used, as well. In the meantime, if I may use this desk, I'll begin writing the story while I wait for a response to my wire."

Rick sat down and began to write...

It was high noon. Two desperate men faced each other down the length of the dusty street. Their women folk were crying on the porch of the general store and wringing their hands.

"I didn't see no women folk."

"It's called artistic license. It was over entirely too fast. I'll have to make it much more exciting for my readers."

"Oh, I see. But ain't that lying?"

"No, the event definitely happened. I shall merely have to embellish the story a bit. Fill in a few details, as it were."

"*Hmm*, sounds like lying to me."

Rick ignored the comment and returned to his task. He was getting used to it.

Evil smiles marred the two faces as the two men advanced steadily toward each other. "You've seen your last sunset," Two-Gun Ace sneered.

"I didn't hear him say that, and he only wore one gun."

"Please. I'll have to ask you to withhold your comments until I'm through writing."

"But what you're writing..." Then he fell silent.

Black Jack laughed a wicked laugh. "Your widow will be putting flowers on your grave before this day is over," he said.

"How'd you hear that? I couldn't hear what they were saying, how could you? And I seriously doubt if..."

"Mr. Powell! I thought we discussed this."

"Yes...yes, I'll be quiet."

Rick stared at the page. "Now you've done it! You've broken my concentration. What do you suppose actually triggered the contest? I mean, how did they know to draw their weapons?"

"Well, how would I know? Instinct, maybe. Perhaps one of them made a move. My guess would be that Black Jack yelled something like, 'Fill yore hand!' as he reached for his gun."

"Fill your hand? How marvelous! May I use that?"

"Of course I don't mind...not if you'll put my name in your book."

Rick smiled as he entered the phrase.

"Fill yore hand!" Black Jack screamed as his hand swept toward the big iron on his hip. But it was not even clear of the holster before he saw the black hole of death spouting fire at the end of the street. He felt the bullets rip

into his body and felt himself falling...falling...his last conscious thought...

"Last conscious thought? You gonna tell me you know what was in the man's mind?"

"I can guess."

"More of that artistic license horse doodle, I suppose."

His last conscious thought was that of his sweetheart, her angel face slowly fading into oblivion as his blood mingled with the dirt in the street.

Rick looked up. "What do you think?"

"I think we done seen two different gun fights. But, here's your wire, and here's your money."

"Thank you, sir, you've been most kind. Now I must go over to buy Mr. Ace his drink. And get permission to use his name in the book."

"And if he doesn't go along with it?"

"Then I shall select a fictitious name, of course. In fact, I think I might call him...Deadwood Dick."

"I wouldn't do that if I were you."

"Why not, pray tell?"

"Because there really is a Deadwood Dick, and if he reads how you're throwing his name around without his permission you're likely to find yourself on the other end of a street with him."

"Oh my, I wouldn't like that." Rick turned to go out the door. He stopped and looked back. "You wouldn't by chance be related to the James family down in South Texas, would you?"

"No, why do you ask?"

"Nothing...nothing at all," but the blue eyes and pigtails of his earlier tormentor were prominent in his thoughts as he turned to go out the door.

Putting the money in his wallet, Rick stepped out and walked over to the saloon. Pushing through the batwing doors, he immediately saw Ace standing at the bar. Men were laughing and patting him on the back.

It would appear successful gunfighters enjoy celebrity status out here, Rick thought as he walked over to the man. "Excuse me, sir, but I believe I owe you a drink."

"That you do, stranger, and I'm right happy to be here to collect. I didn't mean to be short with you out there, but I was a bit preoccupied."

"Yes, I can see where you would be." Rick signaled the bartender who set two mugs of beer before them. "You mind if I ask what provoked this altercation?"

"Altercation? You aren't from around here, are you?"

"No, I'm a writer from back east."

"Figured you for a Yankee. You say you're a writer? You write these dime novels?"

"I do."

"I have one in my room. I don't recall the title, but

it's about a young man riding a wild horse."

"Yes, that would be one of mine. The horse is outside if you would like to make his acquaintance, though I would not recommend trying to mount him."

"Seems like that's what the book said. Are you saying that was you that made that ride?"

"It was."

From his look Rick gathered Ace didn't believe him. "I'm afraid I'm a bit on the stubborn side."

"Yeah...maybe...and maybe you aren't the greenhorn you appear to be."

"Greenhorn?"

"Then again, maybe you are. You gonna write a book about what you saw today?"

"Yes, I think I shall."

"You gonna use real names?"

"Not if you don't wish me to."

"I don't wish you to. I have more reputation now than I desire to have. You see, stranger, the more reputation you have, the more you have to defend it. There's always some young gunhand looking to take it from you."

"I see. Then I won't. I shall have to invent a name."

"Why don't you use Catfish Charlie? I think that'd be an admirable name."

"Is it presently in use?"

"Yes, by an old saloon swamper and professional drunk in Abilene. I don't think gaining reputation will hurt him a bit." He smiled a strange little smile. "Besides, it'll hand a nice laugh to anyone who reads the book and really knows him."

"I like that. Catfish Charlie it is."

"I've thought of using it myself. You see, I've toyed with the idea of writing some."

"I've talked to a lot of people who want to write. Most of them never try. Curious."

"Yes, that's my case as well. I've always thought I could, but I'll probably never try."

"Well I shan't use the name if you anticipate using it yourself."

"No, go ahead. I know I won't."

Suddenly the batwing doors burst open and a man rushed into the room. "*Ace Deadman, you in here?*"

"That would be me."

"I hear tell you shot my cousin."

"And he would be...?"

"Black Jack Wilson."

"Ah yes. If you would be so kind as to await me in the street I will be there shortly." Ace turned to face Rick. "A bit faster than usual, but I suppose now you see what I mean. Once you have a reputation..."

Nine:

The Daring Stagecoach Rescue

Riding along the ridge line, a commotion below caught Rick's attention. He looked to see a stagecoach careening wildly down the road. It appeared to have no driver. He urged Sundown over the edge and down the slope on a course to intercept the speeding coach. As he closed the distance, he heard an occasional scream coming from the inside. It was clearly a woman's voice.

Pulling alongside, he grabbed the trailing reins and began to pull up, holding back on the frightened animal. The horse responded, which slowed the one behind him as well, but there was no restraint on the animals on the other side. This resulted in the team beginning to run in a circle. After a brief period running in steadily diminishing circles, he finally brought them to a halt where they stood panting for breath.

Rick stepped down and opened the door to the coach. There he found a slightly disheveled young lady trying to compose herself. Her hat set askew on her head, covering one eye. She appeared quite shaken. Even shaken up, however, it could not disguise the beauty before him. She had hair that approached burnt copper in color, and before the cloud of red dust arrived he guessed her dress had been maybe an antique white. Her blue eyes in contrast to that red hair were striking.

"Are you all right?" Rick knew it was a foolish question, yet it seemed to be the appropriate thing to ask.

"I think so. You are the one who stopped the horses?"

"I did. Please allow me to introduce myself. I'm Rick Dayton." He swept off his hat. "At your service."

"I am Samantha Gray." She accepted his hand and stepped down from the coach. Her legs seemed to be a bit shaky. He retained his grip on her arm to steady her.

"Could I offer you a drink from my canteen? I'm sorry, I have no cup or container."

"That's quite all right. I can drink straight from it." She took a couple of sips and returned it. "Thank you, I'm feeling better now."

Rick reluctantly released his grip. "How is it you find yourself in the back on an out-of-control stagecoach?"

"It was a holdup. There was a gentleman passenger with me, and of course a driver up on top.

The passenger drew his pistol and it caused both men to get shot. The noise spooked the horses, and well, here I am."

Rick looked inside as she spoke. He pulled his head back out and said, "I'm afraid the passenger is dead."

"I fear the driver is, too, they shot him several times."

"Why didn't the bandits stop the coach?"

"I think they intended to. They chased it for quite a ways, but it gained a substantial lead on them while they were occupied with the driver. They gave up."

"Yes, I'm on quite a horse, and I would have had trouble if I hadn't been able to take an angle to cut them off. They were really moving."

"It was frightening."

Rick climbed up the front wheel to the driver's box. "Well," he looked down at her, "you were quite correct about the driver as well." He jumped down and dusted off his hands. "I suppose the next thing to do is to get you to town."

"I'd be eternally grateful."

"I'm afraid I can't drive a six horse team. But I can't leave them, either."

"Is it so difficult?"

"Yes. I had occasion to interview a stagecoach driver. From his description I would have to say quite difficult. It requires a process of individually controlling six horses at once, alternately encouraging them or pulling back on one or the other reins. It's a matter of working six individual lines up and back in your hands, quite a complicated process. I'm afraid it's one which requires a great deal of practice."

"I had no idea."

"I think I may be able to lead them, however. Though in the event I cannot do so successfully, it might be best if you rode behind me. I'd not like to have to depend on being able to stop the team again, were they to get in their heads to run."

"Yes, that would seem prudent."

They mounted and Rick began to lead the now relatively docile team. The horses seemed to enjoy the chance to walk leisurely instead of their usual rapid pace and came along readily. Having proven this, Samantha could have safely moved back to the comfort of the coach, but neither of them suggested it.

She held on tight, even though the horse was gently walking. "You were so brave, risking yourself to save me that way."

"It was nothing."

"I will never believe that."

"As you wish. Although I am thinking of using it in one of my publications."

"You are a writer?"

"I am."

"How exciting."

"How does *The Daring Stagecoach Rescue* sound to you?"

"I would find it intriguing."

"Then that is what it shall be."

"Will I be in it?"

"You, my dear, will be the heroine. Providing you find it acceptable, of course."

"It would be wonderful. I should be the envy of Charleston when I return."

"I must warn you. Since the event happened so quickly, it will probably be necessary to embellish the story a bit."

"I quite understand. My Uncle Gilbert's stories get larger every time he tells them."

"Ahh, you do understand. Any story worth telling is worth telling well. Perhaps your Uncle will favor me with a story I can use."

The trip back to town was uneventful. In fact, with such delightful company Rick found the time involved far too short. He deposited the team with the Wells Fargo agent, and turned his attention to delivering Miss Samantha to her Uncle Gilbert's home.

Uncle Gilbert turned out to be Gilbert Rowland, president of the Sweetwater Bank & Trust. He was a rotund man, one who carried himself ramrod stiff with his chin held high. He affected full and bushy sideburns, and had a gold watch chain large enough to secure a wagon.

He was delighted to see his niece, and the family accorded Rick with the stature of a full-fledged hero. He was appropriately modest about the accomplishment, but finally agreed to at least take dinner with the family that evening.

The evening proved to be very pleasant, with excellent food second only to the delightful company and lively conversation. Following the meal Mr. Rowland led Rick to the study for a cigar and after dinner drinks while the ladies cleared the table.

"Your niece indicated that you have had quite an exciting life, Mr. Rowland, and that you might have a story or two which might be useful in my writing."

"*Harrumph*, ah yes, I should say so. I have often thought of writing my memoirs. I'm sure I could produce quite an interesting book. It would be a much weightier volume, of course, nothing like the small pamphlets you are writing. No offense, of course."

"None taken, sir. My books are merely fanciful little pieces intended to entertain and amuse."

"Yes, indeed, well when I find the time I'm sure I'll turn my attention to writing something really worthy of the effort. But, I digress, and in the meantime, I suppose sharing a little tale to help you in your effort cannot hurt."

He settled into a chair before he continued. "Sit, my good man, sit. I looked over the book you gave Samantha. Quite fanciful, of course, although I did find the part about the brawl in the bar quite amusing. Yes, singularly amusing."

"I hope you were entertained by it, sir."

"Well, in the light of that story, perhaps you would like to hear about the time my bank was held up."

"I would indeed."

"I remember it as if it were yesterday. It had been a slow morning with virtually no activity in the bank. At such times I often take advantage of the break to further train my employees. I believe strongly in a regimented in-service training program within the organization."

"I see, sir. How many employees do you have?"

"One, Wilbur Townshend. He's my teller, a bright, ambitious young man. I was working with Wilbur on the intricacies of logging and documenting transactions when we glanced up to see two gentlemen entering the building. I immediately suspected something was amiss, primarily because they had kerchiefs drawn over their faces."

"Very observant, sir."

"Had that not given them away, the six-guns they held in their hands almost certainly would have. They demanded that we extend our hands upward and we, of course, complied."

"You must have been terrified."

"On the contrary. I was calm and cool, turning my options over in my head, seeking the means of foiling the brigands in their game."

"Amazing."

"I first thought of the weapon under the counter in the teller's cage. Had it been only Wilbur behind the counter, I would have expected him to pull the weapon and dispatch the robbers before they could reply. However, the community can scarcely afford to lose me, and since the ruffians already had their weapons in their hands, I deemed that an inappropriate risk."

"Of course."

"My second thought was to try and signal for assistance. However, at the bank we leave the shades drawn until the sun is high enough to not shine in the front windows. As the sun had not yet reached its zenith, that move had not been made. I might add, this policy has been re-evaluated and discontinued."

"Very sensible. Do you mind if I make notes as we talk?"

"I should think it would be quite necessary to record it accurately. Now where was I? Oh yes, as I was calmly weighing my options, one of the villains stepped up to the counter and entreated us to back away as the other came around and filled his saddle bags with money. Fortunately the majority of the funds were safely locked in the vault. They noticed it all too soon, however, and I found a gun stuck in my ribs as I was ordered to open the vault door."

"Goodness."

"I told him it was on a time lock and could not be opened until the following morning. He said such a thing would make him very mad and he would be likely to shoot me just for spite. Upon careful consideration I again concluded this to be an imprudent risk and complied with his request. The scoundrels emptied the safe, tied us up, and made a getaway at their leisure. It wasn't until Mrs. McCafferty came in almost an hour later that we were discovered and freed."

"*Tsk, tsk.*"

"Precisely. As soon as I was freed I made my way to the sheriff's office and prevailed on him to immediately gather a posse. I even recommended the individuals I was sure would consent to serve. I went with the posse, of course, to protect my interests."

"Naturally."

"We had two days of hard riding, staying on the outlaws trail. I'll admit it took a toll on me. I'm not used to roughing it in such a manner. Members of the posse also found it exhausting and were ready to turn back. I prevailed upon them to persevere."

"I see. You raised the reward?"

"What reward? I told them if they didn't stay after it I was going to call in their loans and mortgages."

"Nothing like the proper motivation."

"My thoughts exactly. We followed their trail into the town of Sand Springs. As soon as we hit town, we split up to search for them. I feared they were up to their old tricks, and the sheriff and I made directly for the bank. It was as I had thought. We walked into the bank to find them seated across from the bank president, Sam Tucker. The sheriff leveled his gun on them and ordered them not to move.

"Sam looked up at me and said, 'Hello, Gilbert,

what are you doing way down here?' I said I was chasing bank robbers, but told him I saw he had already made their acquaintance."

He said, 'Bank robbers? No, there must be some mistake. These gentlemen run a little ranch south of town. I'm sorry to say they got far behind on their payments, but have prevailed on some relatives for help and are here to settle the debt.'

"'Relatives, balderdash,' I said, 'that money came from my bank at the point of a gun.'

"'Robbed one bank to pay off another? Gilbert, that's preposterous!'

"'Preposterous, is it? Sheriff, do your duty.' As the sheriff escorted the bad men away, I sat down to negotiate with Sam over the possession of the funds. He was quick to point out that until the men were convicted of a crime, the money was legally deposited in his bank. I am afraid we disagreed on the subject. Finally we reached an accommodation where half would remain in each facility until such a time as the disposition of the case would occur."

"My, Mr. Rowland. That's an incredible story. I fear I cannot do it justice in a book, though I shall certainly try."

The door to the study pulled apart slightly and a pair of soft blue eyes peered in. Samantha said, "Have you gentlemen finished your 'man talk'? My aunt says I may not take a walk around town without a male escort."

Rick jumped to his feet. "I should be honored to perform such a service."

She smiled, and they walked out to take the night air. She said, "Did Uncle Gilbert give you something you can use?"

"He certainly did. I think it will make an excellent story. I am considering calling it, *Bank Merger— Western Style*. What do you think?"

Ten:

They Call Them Buffalo Soldiers

Sundown and I have been following the bright, sparkling stream for hours. When we started, the Davis Mountains were dim shadows in the distance. Now they are progressively higher on either side of us, and we are surrounded by trees and bushes shouting with the bright colors of autumn.

Rick stopped writing in his journal and patted the big horse on the neck. "Shouting with the colors of autumn. You like that, Sundown? Kinda has a ring to it, doesn't it?"

Sundown tossed his head as if to indicate he had heard. He liked for Rick to talk to him, but he seldom had any critique to offer on his writing. Actually, Rick supposed that using the word *seldom* was being a little generous.

He continued to write:

Fort Davis and these mountains both got

their name from the same person, Jefferson Davis, while he was the Secretary of War, not after he became President of the Confederacy. It's a bit surprising that they didn't come back and change the name after that happened, particularly the name of the fort. Having a Union fort named after a Confederate leader is a bit strange, after all.

Rick looked up just long enough to confirm he was still on course, then returned to writing.

This creek is Limpia Creek, which I understand means "clean" in Spanish. Doesn't take but one look to understand why.

He glanced up again; the steep slopes of the mountains were beginning to recede, opening out into a valley. He saw the fort stretch out before him, a collection of long narrow buildings around a common parade ground. Beyond it were a few small buildings, which appeared to be the beginnings of a town. He tucked the journal into his saddlebags and rode toward an adobe structure flying a US flag and the flag of the Ninth Calvary. Rick took it to be the headquarters building.

As he approached, there was a tall black man leaning against a post on the porch. He wore the triple chevrons of a sergeant, and the high riding boots of a cavalryman. He straightened up as Rick approached, and spoke in a friendly fashion. "Morning Sah." His deep bass voice and rich southern drawl stretched the word and gave it a musical sound.

Rick gave him a smile. "Is this the post headquarters?"

"Yes, sah, Ninth Calvary. I'm Sergeant Carver. You wanna see the colonel?"

"I'd like that."

He stepped inside, coming back almost immediately to say, "The colonel will see you now."

Rick entered and was surprised to find the officer rather a young man wearing the Eagles of a full colonel. He stood behind his desk as Rick entered.

The colonel said, "We don't get many visitors out this way." There was an enthusiasm in his voice, and in some manner Rick was aware of a high energy level coming from him. He had a dark moustache and close cut wavy hair of the same shade. His posture suggested he was accustomed to being obeyed.

Rick extended his hand. "I'm Rick Dayton. I'm a writer. I'm out here in search of material for a book."

The colonel gave him a firm handshake. "Pleased to meet you Mister Dayton. I'm Colonel Edward Hatch, the post commander. I'm sorry to say I've never read anything you've written that I can remember."

"Actually I write under the name of Texas Jack."

"Ah, now I do have several of those little books.

Very interesting, though a little imaginative, if I might say so."

"Yes, they are intended to be entertaining, and any story worth telling is worth telling well."

"Perhaps you will autograph them for me."

"I should be delighted."

While Rick wrote a brief sentiment in the colonel's book, the officer stood over his shoulder and said, "I've always intended to write a book using my military exploits."

Rick closed the last book. What he said was hardly a new thing. "Then you should, Colonel. May I be honest with you?

"Please do."

"Colonel, most of the people I meet tell me they plan to or have wanted to write a book as soon as they hear I'm a writer. Many of them who think so do not have it in them, unfortunately. On the other hand, some great books will never be written because the one and only person who could give it to us never puts it down on paper."

"I see what you mean."

"There's only one requirement to become a writer, and that is to write."

"I can't seem to get started."

"If I may be so bold, perhaps that's because you expect to sit down and write the story straight through from the beginning. Writing seldom works that way, particularly on a first book. More likely, we write pieces and collect facts and thoughts. Often we write the middle before we begin the book, sometimes even starting a tale with the ending we wish to achieve. Don't worry about writing the perfect opening, it'll come."

"But what if I'm one of those who really can't write?"

"Anyone can write. Some can't write well enough to become published, but if that's the case you'll find it out. Worst case, however, is that you will have some wonderful written memories to pass on to your children or family. That in itself is worth doing, is it not?"

"Yes. Yes, it is. Thank you, Mister Dayton."

"Please call me Rick."

"And I'm Edward...Ed. Though I would appreciate being called *Colonel* in front of the men. Discipline, you understand."

"I do, and changing the subject, I won't write a book here if it in any way impedes you from tackling the one you have in mind."

"Actually, I would love you to write one. It is a subject dozens of writers could hardly exhaust."

"I see."

"Do you? I'm not so sure. You see, Rick, this is a Negro Regiment. Actually, we seldom refer to race on this post at all, but if it is required they prefer to be called *black*."

"I wondered when I met your sergeant outside."

"A very good man. To continue, I have ten companies of cavalry and am responsible for this post and for Fort Stockton as well."

"I came through there. Quite an area to be responsible for."

"Our primary duties entail guarding the Butterfield stagecoach stations and route. We have to protect the telegraph line, and settlers."

"Protect them from what?"

"Ah, there's no shortage of potential adversaries. Out here we are the only law that exists, so we must provide domestic law enforcement as well as military action. Our most formidable opponents are the Cheyenne and several bands of Apache. But we are not limited to that, we also have horse and cattle rustlers, carpetbagger politicians, land barons, crooked government contractors, and corrupt Indian agents. We have a variety of Mexican revolutionaries, train and stagecoach robbers, and, given our particular racial mixture, often a hostile press and even the public at large."

"The people you are working to protect?"

"Precisely."

"That must be hard on morale."

"Some, but a majority of my men are used to prejudice. It's a way of life for them. Still, you can see why I wish to tell their story, and no amount of books could be too many. The press and the public at large would rather pretend they didn't even exist."

"I'm your man then. How do we start?" Rick had come here looking for a story. Now he felt as if the young colonel had enlisted him in a cause.

"Excellent. Let's take a tour of the post. You can interview some of the men."

They started across the parade ground. A number of soldiers were drilling, and though it was relatively early in the day, the heat already climbed steadily. Rick asked, "Are all of the officers white?"

"Yes. And this is an unusual assignment for them. Our troopers are strong and brave, but they have no education at all, and are often used to having every little decision made for them. We work at educating them, but know more about them than one would usually know about their men because we write their letters for them and read the responses. We read to them a lot, and I'm sure you'll be happy to know your books are a favorite. They'll be very pleased to meet you."

This was a new feeling for Rick. He had run into someone now and then who had read one of his books, but this was different. He said it. "I have to admit I'm very flattered. I don't know what to say."

A young lieutenant came to attention on the porch as they approached. He saluted.

Colonel Hatch said, "Lt. Meyerson, this is Mr. Dayton." A curious smile came over his face. "Actually, this is Texas Jack Hammer."

"No kidding!" He came out of his military posture

and began to pump Rick's hand. "Man, we read your books all the time. This is great!"

He stopped the pumping action to peer at Rick closely, retaining the grip on his hand. "Somehow I thought you'd be bigger, more..."

Rick retrieved his hand. "I must be a disappointment in real life."

The grin returned. He seemed hardly more than a boy. "Oh no, not in the least. Just wasn't what I pictured, that's all."

Colonel Hatch asked, "Where are the troops, Lieutenant?"

The military bearing returned as if someone had thrown a switch. "The new recruits are drilling, sir, as you can see. We have the usual detail out guarding the herd, and the post guards, of course. There's a fatigue detail up at the sawmill. Lieutenant Cusak is still out on patrol with F Troop as you ordered. Then we have the usual kitchen patrol, some men working over in the stable, and some off duty men have gone out riding."

"In sufficient number, I presume?"

"Yes, sir."

"You see, Rick, the Indians covet our horses terribly. That's why we maintain such a strong guard on the herd, and why we don't allow riding for pleasure unless in enough strength that it doesn't offer a temptation."

"Yet I rode in alone."

"It wasn't the smartest thing you've done lately.

You were lucky."

Rick suddenly felt very hot. He knew he must have a flushed face.

"We'll see that you do not run such a risk as you leave." His stern face melted as he said, "but from your book, I understand there is little chance your horse could be stolen by an Indian. If what you wrote is true."

"It is, but if I understand you correctly I might have not been around to take pleasure in that fact."

The stern look returned. "Yes, there is that, all right."

There was a bit of an awkward silence before Rick asked, "Is there some sort of patrol I might go out with?"

"I don't know about that. It's pretty safe here at the fort, but our patrols often come under fire."

"So, by helping you to tell the story of these men you want me to portray the drilling and the washing pots and pans and such?"

"I thought you'd just interview them and get what you needed."

"Would you be able to write the book you intend to do if you were restricted to that?"

"Point well made. Lieutenant, do we have any other details which might suffice?"

"Sergeant Stance is taking a detail to escort the stage."

"That would be Sergeant Emanuel Stance. Good

man, and I think a fine choice. Very well, Mr. Dayton, against my better judgment."

Stance was leading a detail of four men. Rick mounted and met them at the gate. Introductions were made and they rode out in a column of twos. Rick rode beside the sergeant, a lean, muscular man who looked as if he had been hewn from a single piece of Mahogany.

After they had ridden a short way Stance looked at Rick and said, "You know they call us Buffalo soldiers?"

"No, I hadn't heard that. Why?"

He pulled off his hat. "It's this short nappy hair, that and the fact that we're colored dark like a buffalo. It was cold when we first got here and most of us were wearing buffalo coats. Them Indians hadn't ever seen anything like us before."

"You don't find that offensive?"

"Naw, they don't mean it that way. Just trying to see us in terms they understand. We gotta lotta respect for each other."

One of the soldiers behind spoke up, "Sarge, you see that little smoke sign over there?"

Stance pulled up. "No, I hadn't. Thanks. How about we wait here while you slip over there and take a look-see?"

The soldier spurred his mount toward the thin wisp of smoke. The detail dismounted and gave their horses a rest. It was about ten minutes before the man returned.

"It's a small camp of Cheyenne," he said.

"Hunting or on the warpath?"

"Didn't see nuthin they'd shot, but Sarge, they got two young white boys with them."

"White boys, you sure?"

"Seen 'em plain as day."

"That's too bad, I intended to ride around them. How many did you make it?"

"I'd say fifteen or twenty."

"How were they armed?"

"I saw a few old rifles, but mostly bows and arrows or lances."

"Okay, guess we've got it to do." He looked at Rick. "The colonel told me to try to skirt any serious trouble, but I guess this changes things. I'd leave you here, but I think you'll be in less danger with us."

Rick said he wanted to do his part. They all checked their weapons, then mounted and headed for the smoke at a walk, not anxious for trouble.

The patrol stopped at the bottom of the hill. The camp was over the ridge line. Stance told Rick to stay with the horses, and when he objected Stance explained his inexperience would be more of a liability than a help going into the camp.

"The only chance we got is surprise," he said. "We gotta hit 'em hard and fast and get out before they can get organized. Jackson said they got no guards out, so we have a shot at it. But if they get our mounts we're dead meat, so you have to stay here and guard them. You can do it from the ridge so you can give us cover fire as well. When we come back we're gonna have our tail feathers on fire, so you be ready."

The troopers removed their swords and scabbards and anything else that might rattle and left them on their saddles with their hats. Rick crawled with them to the top and took a bead on the village with his rifle as they slipped down toward the camp. He watched them get closer and closer, then one man split to approach the camp from the other side. They hadn't taken their carbines, but had their revolvers at the ready.

Suddenly Rick saw smoke from Stance's revolver, and an Indian wearing a lot of feathers pitched back as the sound reached him. The other two troopers with him opened fire and they jumped up and charged the camp yelling like banshees. The Indians were temporarily disoriented. Some ran, some took cover, some died reaching for their weapons or trying to return fire. Quietly, on the left flank Corporal Jackson slipped forward, cut the bonds on the two boys, and spirited them quietly into the brush. He sent them running in Rick's direction, then took a position to give cover fire to his comrades.

Their revolvers empty, the three troopers ran from the camp, loading shells into the guns as they ran. Whooping Indians began to give chase. As the warriors ran around the corner of the trail the Corporal emptied his revolver into the first ones to come into view. At the same time Rick began to fire on them as well.

Jackson turned to run as the Indians hesitated again. Stance ran by Rick scooping up a young boy and yelling for everybody to come running. They were barely in the saddle when Jackson ran up and vaulted over the back of his horse to land in the saddle, immediately putting spurs to the animal. The patrol rode down the ridge and out of range as the Indians made the top and fired a few ineffectual shots.

"They'll be after us," Rick said.

"Maybe," the sergeant said, but they've got to run all the way back down to their horses first. I don't figure them to be able to make up the difference."

The patrol rode hard for several miles, then dismounted to give the horses a breather. "It'll have to be a short one," Stance said, "but if we ride these horses to death, we'll be in the stew for sure."

They walked in silence for a couple of minutes before Rick said, "I never shot a man before."

Stance tried to read my face. "You figure you did?"

"I sure enough shot at them."

"Well, maybe you did or maybe you didn't, but you sure enough helped slow them down and that was enough."

"You don't think I did?"

"Your first two shots were pretty long range. You'd have had to been pretty lucky. After that...well, let me put it like this, after you work the lever on that rifle you have to pull the trigger before you work the lever again to really do any good."

"You mean I..."

"There were live rounds laying all around you."

This time Rick knew his face was red, he could feel it. "You must think I..."

"What I think is that all of us have trouble in our first action. You done all right, you hear?"

"Thanks."

"It ain't gonna save you from a little friendly rawhiding, though. You understand? I ain't the only one what seen them bullets."

"I deserve it, and I've been rawhided before."

"I'll bet you have, the way you travel around."

The sergeant turned and gave the order to mount. "Let's get these boys back to safety." He looked at the nearest, a tossle-headed blond about seven or eight. "That all right with you, son?"

The boy just nodded. He was obviously still in shock. Rick looked at him and pulled his journal out. Time to begin the story. He wrote, *They Call Them Buffalo Soldiers.*

Eleven:

The Ambush

Riding alone into Fort Davis had been a mistake. Rick did not repeat it on the way out. Again Sergeant Stance had the duty to meet and escort the Butterfield stagecoach. Rick rode beside him on the way out, followed by the same four troopers. They would intersect the stage down below the mountains, relieve the detail from Fort Stockton, and escort the stage to Pecos. There would be little if any danger from that point on into El Paso.

The patrol topped out a rise to see a dust plume in the distance. The sergeant pulled his field glasses to confirm that it was the approaching stage. He said it was, then continued scanning the countryside.

After a few minutes he said, "Well, I'll be."

"What's up, Sarge?" Jackson asked.

"Sneaky redskins, that's what's up." He passed the glasses to the corporal. "Look in those boulders there at that little pass."

Then they passed the field glasses to Rick. He looked and saw nothing. It took some prodding, and movement by one of the Indians before he saw anything.

"Oh, yes I see."

"I make it to be Mescalero Apache, Jackson, you agree?" Stance said. "Maybe a dozen?"

"That's what I figure. The coach is too far away to hear a warning shot, and if they ride in cold turkey them boys from M Troop is likely to be caught with their pants down."

"Looks like we got it to do again, don't it?" He looked at Rick. "Don't guess I could talk you into meeting the stage over on the other side of that pass."

Rick told him that he had a little something to make up for and wanted the chance to do it.

"Spect I'd do the same thing in your boots. Okay, boys, we gotta leave the horses over there, and slip up on them easy like. Real slow, because if we roll one rock down on them it'll be us in the soup instead of those boys from M Troop."

The patrol tied off the horses and made their way slowly to a position just above the Indians. The coach was visible now, the cavalry detail following closely.

"Why aren't the cavalry in front?" Rick asked.

"We never ride in front because that would make the civilians eat our dust. Be bad public relations."

"How bad will the public relations be if the Indians shoot them right in front of the troopers?"

"Won't happen that way. They'll let the stage slide right through and ambush the patrol. They know afterwards they can always chase that stage down."

"So, we're their only chance?"

"No, them boys from Stockton are pretty salty. They might get the job done even if we weren't here. I'd like to think we would if we were in their boots. But it'd be pretty messy. This way is better."

The sergeant pulled his hat off and moved into firing position. He said, "Pick you some targets boys, when that stage goes through them Apaches will come out to fire and we'll have to be ready. Won't be no time to pick and choose, so take what you can get a bead on."

Things seemed to go into slow motion. Through the dust and the heat waves, the horses appeared to float. Sweat ran into their eyes, and a fly buzzed Rick's face, but he was afraid to brush either for fear his movement would be seen by those waiting below.

The slow motion ended and the coach swept through the pass in a blur. As the patrol thundered behind them, the Apache swarmed out to take firing positions. As they did the troopers behind them fired almost as one. Rick had picked an Indian wearing a headband but who was naked to the waist. As he pulled the trigger he saw him spin away and saw the crimson on his chest. No doubt this time. There were no unspent shells flying away either as Rick took his time, sighting and firing.

The Apache turned from their intended victims and began to move on those behind them, returning the fire. The air sounded like it was full of angry wasps. The noise of those rounds passing seemed to not be connected to the explosions of the guns below. The whole thing did not appear to be real. It was a disjointed dream as Rick again found his sights on the face of an Indian peering at him over his own rifle. Rick fired first and he disappeared.

Suddenly the guns of M Troop came into play and caught the hostiles in a crossfire. More fell, and the remaining Indians disappeared as if they had never been there at all.

The mounted patrol rode looking for stragglers, but found none. The patrol Rick was with retrieved their horses, said their goodbyes, and Rick rode to catch up with the stage which had slowed up to see the results of the action. He wasn't sure he wanted to think back on what he had done long enough to write it. Maybe there wouldn't be a book called *The Ambush*.

Twelve:

The World's First Rodeo

The remainder of the trip was uneventful, and it seemed no time before they were on the outskirts of Pecos. As they entered town they headed straight for the Orient Saloon. For the first time in Rick's life he really felt in need of a drink, and not just because he was thirsty.

Sipping on the almost-cool beer, Rick finally felt some of the tension leave. Still, it was a number of further sips before he became aware enough of his surroundings enough to know what all the animated discussions were all about. It seemed a number of cowboys from surrounding ranches were strongly disagreeing as to who had the best riders and ropers.

"Ain't no two ways about it," a cowboy said, "everybody knows our boss man at the Lazy Y is greased lightening with a rope."

"Aw, he can't hold a candle to Morg Livingston over to the Hashknife," someone answered.

"Or Fate Beard...maybe Henry Slack..." other voices added.

It was a discussion that seemed to have no resolution in sight. "Ought to have a contest to prove who is right," Rick suggested.

"Now there's an idea," someone answered. "I've got a little money I'd wager on such an event."

"Why should I wear a good roping horse out just so you guys can bet on it? You know I don't favor gambling." The man next to Rick told him the speaker, Trav Windham, was the odds on favorite for the roping title.

The bartender said, "How about it, stranger, it was your idea."

"It wouldn't be gambling if there were prize money involved. That's what a contest is usually for, prize money. I'd say each contestant would put up an entry fee, then the winner would take all."

"There you go," the bartender said. "That's the answer, Trav, you wouldn't be gambling, just competing for prize money. And I'd be willing to put up forty dollars added money just to sweeten the pot."

"*Forty dollars!*" Livingston grinned. "Say, that shines, that's near three months pay."

The saloon emptied as the contest moved out into the street next to the courthouse. Several hands went to get steers to use in the contest. Rick pulled out his journal:

These are not calves, but quarter of a ton range animals with menacing horns and fire in their eyes.

No feedlot creatures these.

By the time the animals were gathered, a sizable crowd had crowded the courthouse square. Since it was the Fourth of July all the families were in town, and a big barbecue was slated for later in the afternoon.

A loose arena was formed of freight wagons and spring wagons. The big animals were loose held behind the wagons and sent barreling into the street one at a time as the cowboys called for them.

Rick continued to write:

"Let me have him" the man said, and the huge animal burst through between the wagons, propelled by slaps of a rope that startled him into a full run. Bending low over his horse's neck, Windham put spurs to his horse and the animal literally exploded into a run hard on the cows heels. Two quick circles around his head with the lariat and the loop settled over the nick of the big steer. The horse stopped so abruptly that he nearly sat down, and the man was off him and in a run for the cow before the horse slid to a stop. A peggin' string came from between his teeth and he tied three of the animal's legs in a motion so fast I couldn't discern how he made the knot. He threw his hand up and stepped back.

"Twenty one seconds," the timekeeper announced.

"Say, that'll be hard to beat," the man next to Rick said.

It turned out it was. Dust flew, cowboys and animals alike sweat and tried, but the time stood. Along with the prize money, Trav Windham was awarded the blue ribbon, which came from the dress of an attractive young girl. She presented it with a kiss for his cheek, and a tradition was born.

Thirteen:

God's Cathedral

Rick met Jim White at the Butterfield stage stop. He was a working hand on the XXX spread owned by the Lucas brothers. Ranging out from headquarters, he'd come by the stage stop to get a hot meal. "My name is Rick Dayton."

He had a shy smile and favored Rick with a little of it as he extended a hand. He was a tall, unassuming man and wore a white shirt and faded jeans. "I'm Jim White. I ride for the Triple X."

Coming through wiping his hands, the horse hostler said, "He's a writer, Jim. Writes these here adventure books."

White gave Rick an appraising look, as if he were measuring him for something. "You don't say. Afraid I don't read much. Never had no formal schoolin'. Whatcha doing up this way?"

Rick told him he was traveling, looking for stories.

He said, "I sure enough got a story."

"Really? Tell me about it."

"It ain't so much for the telling as it is for the

showing. You finish up that stew and we'll go take a look-see."

After lunch they rode out towards a ridge of mountains to the northwest. He said they were the Guadalupes. He pointed toward the tallest, the southernmost part of the range. "That there is El Capitan. It's a big'un."

But Rick's attention was drawn further north. "Something's on fire over there."

He chuckled softly. "That's what we come to see."

"A fire?"

"You know, I figured it to be a volcano when I first seen it. Not that I ever saw a volcano, but that was what come to mind."

Rick shook his head. "Now it looks more like a tornado to me."

"Never seen one of them neither."

The cloud didn't move, but continued to spin in one place as they moved toward it. Over a half hour of riding and still it didn't move.

"That's not smoke," Rick finally said. "That's something flying in the air. What on earth is it?"

"Bats. Millions of them."

"Bats? I can't believe it."

"Believe it. Before I run into this place I couldn't imagine a million of anything. Too big a number to wrap my mind around. But now I know what a million bats looks like."

"This is amazing."

They worked their way through rocks and brush until they reached a point where they could look down into a huge hole. The bats continued to emerge in a solid formation. The air was filled with an unusual sound–the whisper of millions of wings.

They'd come out of the darkness and begin to spiral around the opening until they finally got their bearings and flew off to the southeast, the lowest point in the surrounding hills.

"I reckoned any cave big enough to hold all these critters must be some hole."

"You've been in there?"

"Sure have. That's your story. I'm gonna take you in."

Rick shuddered at the thought of going in where all these flying rodents lived. He told the man so.

"Aw, bats won't hurt you. You hear all these stories about them, but they ain't dangerous to nothing but mosquitoes and moths. They sure keep them cleaned up, though."

It started to get dark. "Won't we have to wait until daylight?"

"Mister, night or day it don't make much difference down there."

"How do we get in?"

"Won't be as hard as when I first went. You see, I done made me this ladder out of fence wire with sticks for steps. Got some coal oil torches stashed down there, too. We'll use these lanterns until we get to them."

"Why are you doing this?"

"Down there is the most amazing thing I ever saw, but folks around here figure me for crazy. I ain't been able to talk one single cowboy into going down with me. Reckon if you were to write about it, folks might want to come see it. I tell you, mister, people ought to see this."

"And you think I'm crazy enough to go see it?"

"You wanted a story."

"You're right. I'm crazy enough."

They started down the ladder and Rick began to wonder if he really was crazy enough. The ladder swung and swayed, and when he looked down what he saw was like peering into the entrance to Hell itself. It was the blackest black he had ever seen, like a solid thing, as if he could step onto it and stand. The lanterns they had with us barely cast a glow, but were absorbed by the dark.

The ladder ended up on a narrow ledge, and they had to hug the wall and inch or way over to a level floor. As they eased forward, the tunnel grew larger and larger.

The pair got to the place where White had the torches cached. "Find yourself a spot and hold still. You got to see this...or maybe I should say, not see this."

Rick sat down on a ledge.

"I'm gonna turn this lantern off before I light these torches."

As he extinguished the lanterns, a darkness closed on them such as Rick had never experienced before. It seemed to have substance, like tons of black wool. He held his hand in front of his face, but even though he touched his own nose, he could see nothing.

And the quiet. It was unearthly. Then he started to hear sounds. Rick heard...church chimes...or maybe sleigh bells...what was that?

White got a torch lit and saw a bat flying among the stalagmites, its wings striking them, making a resounding tone.

White nodded his head towards it. "Each of them things has a different tone. They're called stalagmites. I've read about them but have never seen any. The ones that hang down from overhead are called stalactites."

"Is that right? Say, I'm glad to know that. How do you remember which is which?"

"Easy, G for the ground and C for the ceiling."

"Okay, I can remember that." Rick would have to remember it; it was far too dark to make notes in his journal.

They spoke quietly, as if in church, yet their voices echoed all around them, over and over again.

"It's chilly," Rick said.

"Got a thermometer around here somewhere. Always the same in here, day or night, summer or winter. Fifty-six degrees."

"That's amazing."

Rick's eyes began to adjust to the light and he began to see a fairyland of complex formations surrounding them. And it was huge! The shadows played on the wall, casting ghostly shapes. The little furry creatures flying among them made the scene even spookier.

"You're right, this is a story, but I don't know how I'm going to do it justice."

"How's that?"

"As I climbed down I thought I was descending into Hell. Now I see it's more the opposite. This is God's handiwork. Man could never make a cathedral this beautiful. In fact, that's what I think I'll call my story, *God's Cathedral*."

Fourteen:

The Jail Break

The jail in Lincoln County, New Mexico was on the second floor above the sheriff's office. Rick had been given the opportunity to talk to one of the most famous killers in history, Billy the Kid. With the Kid set to hang the following morning, this was sure to be his last interview.

When Rick arrived the Kid was playing cards with Deputy J.W. Bell. He was hampered by the manacles on his hands. Rick wouldn't have said it to Billy's face, but he was a singularly homely young man, with buckteeth and a slight build. Not at all what Rick had expected. He had expected somebody larger than life.

Rick sat against the wall and began to ask questions. The Kid paid little attention, but focused his attention on the card game as if they played for more than matches.

Rick wrote in his journal:

The most notorious shootist in the West appears to be but a boy, a very plain young man, extremely quiet and reserved. Hardly what one would expect for one said to have killed a man for every year of his life, twenty-one.

He stopped writing and asked if the statement about the number of men he had killed was true. Billy gave him a sideways glance. "You expect me to answer a question like that right in front of a deputy sheriff? You ain't as smart as I took you for."

"Aw, Billy," Bell said, "you're gonna hang in the morning anyway. You ought to tell your story to the man."

Rick waved his comment aside. "That's all right. He certainly doesn't have to answer any questions he doesn't wish to respond to. How did you get started in a life of crime, Billy?"

A flash of anger came into the boy's eyes. "I don't consider myself involved in a life of crime as you put it. I ain't had no choice in the way things have come about. But as to what happened first, I reckon you'd have to lay that at the door of a no account by the name of Sombrero Jack up Silver City way. Never did know his last name. He made me hide a bunch of stolen laundry. The sheriff put me in jail when he found it and I wouldn't snitch on who really done it. I fooled him, though, I crawled through the chimney and escaped." He snickered. "I've escaped a lot."

"How old were you, Billy?"

"Then? I was fifteen. There was a poster put out on me after the escape and I took to calling myself Henry. Henry Antrim."

"Is that when you killed your first man?"

"Told you I didn't want to talk about that," he snapped. Then he glanced at Bell and more softly said, "Aw, maybe you're right. What have I got to lose? There was this guy named Windy Cahill there in Silver City. He was the camp blacksmith and a real bully. I didn't move fast enough to suit him one day and he flung me to the ground and took to whomping on me. I pulled his own gun outta his belt and shot him. Funny, that was the first time I ever shot a gun."

"Surely that was self-defense."

"Before he died he had people write out a statement that I figured ought to clear me, but they threw me in the post stockade and was gonna hang me. Out here in the West, they think anybody old enough to kill is old enough to hang. But I escaped."

"Amazing! What happened then?"

"I roamed around Arizona and the Indian Territory for a while, then I got caught up in the Lincoln County war. We all done some killing in that. Don't understand why I should be singled out..."

He reached out to place a wager of ten matches into the pot, but in the process knocked a card to the floor. It was the Jack of Hearts.

"Didn't mean to do that, Bell. Hard to play with handcuffs on."

"That's all right, Kid." Bell bent to pick up the card. His head was below the top of the table for a fraction of a second. It was enough.

The Kid moved like a snake, pulling the deputy's gun. Bell raised back up to look down the muzzle of his own weapon. Rick held his breath.

"Do what I tell you, Bell, and be mighty quick about it." Billy's voice was crisp and sharp. "Don't make a false move. You're a dead man if you do. I don't want to kill you. You've been good to me. Turn around and walk out the door. I'm gonna lock you in the armory." He looked at Rick. "You, too."

The trio turned and marched out the door. Rick could hear the Kid shuffle behind them in his leg irons.

There's no telling why Bell did what he did then. Maybe his pride was hurt. The Kid had been sitting there talking about all of his escapes, yet here they were. Possibly couldn't bear the thought of having to explain to Sheriff Pat Garrett how he had been tricked.

Whatever the reason, they came to the head of the back stairs, almost to the armory door, with the Kid maybe five or six feet behind them. Bell must have thought the wall would shield him long enough as he suddenly made his move. He started to take the steps three at a time. Rick jerked back against the wall.

The Kid was just too quick. The bullet took Bell under the left shoulder blade, cutting through his heart. Rick turned and found himself looking straight into the eyes of death.

They held each other's eyes for an eternity, then unexpectedly Billy grinned. "You see what I mean? It ain't ever my fault. Didn't have to happen like this."

He jammed Bell's gun into his belt and caught up a double-barreled shotgun from the armory.

"You can just wipe that sweat off your forehead. If I shoot you, who's gonna tell my story? You get yourself back into that jail and stay put. You poke as much as your nose out here and I'm gonna blow it off, though."

Rick didn't need any further encouragement. Billy apparently paused and used Bell's keys to remove the shackles, because moments later Rick looked out the window to see he wasn't wearing them running down the back steps.

Rick saw him cut down Deputy Bob Olinger with what he found out later was Olinger's own shotgun. The Kid jumped on a horse and rode off.

Rick sat down abruptly, suddenly shaking too bad to stand. It made no sense to him that he was still alive.

Fifteen:

Cowboy Camp Meeting

Back East, the perception of the West was wild and woolly. Hard drinking, hard gambling cowboys fighting and cussing and spending a month's pay in one night. There was a lot of truth in this perception, but Rick also discovered a less visible but very sizable percentage of people out here to be homebodies, family oriented people with a solid moral base and strong religious convictions.

Still, churches and preachers were rare, and when a circuit rider came through it was very well attended. It was called a camp meeting, with singing and dinner on the grounds. He knew those who consumed the dime novels wanted action and excitement, and doubted this would result in a book he could sell. But then again, while he wrote for immediate consumption, perhaps he'd start a longer work, a study of these people, how they lived and worked...and worshiped.

But more than anything else Rick missed his regular church attendance and looked forward to the experience from a personal point of view.

He met three XIT chuck wagons on their way on the way to the meeting, plus one from the LS.

He rode into the camp to see ladies working around fires all over the clearing. Any get-together in this country was occasion for a feast and this would apparently be no exception. A lady welcomed him.

"Hello there. I'm Janie Benedict. I haven't seen you here before."

She had a pleasant smile and extended a hand. When Rick took it, he found it surprisingly hard. She had on a simple dress covered by a full apron. Strands of hair escaped the tight bun obviously intended to keep her hair out of her way as she cooked.

"No, I haven't been here before. I'm Rick Dayton. I'm supposed to tell you there are chuck wagons at the stream filling their water barrels, ma'am. They said not to worry about the coffee, they'll take care of it. They also said Mr. Campbell of the XIT had sent them to put on some beeves to cook to go along with your fixin's."

"Why, how generous."

"I'm told the gentleman's nickname is Barbecue Campbell, apparently not without cause."

"They intend to furnish the meat as well?"

"That's what they said.

"Janie, what is the timing on this?" a voice behind us said. The lady turned and introduced me to Reverend Graham, who acknowledged the introduction before he continued. "I've selected a little hillside over by the stream. There's a substantial rock for me to stand on at the bottom where I may be heard. It looks like a wonderful success. There must be forty or fifty people there waiting."

The reverend was beaming. He was a slight man and seemed to have been swallowed by the black frock coat that was the hallmark of his profession. He held a large black Bible and patted it comfortingly as he talked.

Janie smiled a patient smile at the man. "Forty to fifty, Reverend, we expect more than ten times that number."

"What! But I've never...I mean, not even in...Oh, my, what a triumph for the Lord!"

"What will you preach about?" Rick asked.

"I've started over five times. I'm afraid I don't have any skill as an evangelist. I'm used to a congregation who already knows the Bible, and we study it together."

"There may be a lot here today who know the Bible, but the ones who don't are the ones you need to reach the most, don't you agree?"

"Yes, I certainly do. Believe me, I know what needs to be done, but I'm so nervous. I simply can't waste this wonderful opportunity."

She patted on the arm. "Don't worry, you'll be fine. You'll be given the words to say. Just keep it simple. Simply tell them what they have to do to be saved."

He looked relieved. "Yes, you're right, of course. It's ever bit that simple, isn't it?"

Several beeves soon cooked on open pits by the ranch chuck wagons. Big pots of coffee were on fires around the area and all of the wagons, Janie's as well as the others, were full of pies and steaming vegetables. There was a piece missing here and there, since cooks are accustomed to eating as they prepare the food.

Near the stream the hillside was covered with people, and they had prevailed upon Brother Graham to get started. They could easily hear his ringing voice over at the wagons, and the cooks paused often to listen. He took his text from Isaiah Chapter 55.

He read, "Ho, every one that thirsteth come ye to the waters," he gestured to the stream at his feet, "and he that hath no money, come ye, buy and eat; yea, come, buy wine and milk without money and without price."

He looked up. "Isn't it amazing God could cause words to be written thousands of years ago, words that say exactly what is happening today? But God knows the future. He knew even then we would be gathered here awaiting those mouth-watering pies and that good barbecued beef."

He read on. "Wherefore do you spend money for that which is not bread? And your labour for that which satisfyeth not? Harken diligently unto me, and eat ye that which is good, and let your soul delight itself in fatness.

"It couldn't be more clear if the Lord had written you a personal letter, which is actually what much of the Bible is. Did you ever think of it that way? The Lord knew you were going to be here right now at this time, and *He* caused a message to be written for me to give to you. What do we spend money on which doesn't sustain us? What do we spend our time and effort doing which doesn't fulfill us? You don't need me to tell you that, because the answer is written on your heart."

Reading again, he said, "Incline your ear and come unto me; hear and your soul will live and I will make an everlasting covenant with you."

He looked up and smiled. "That's good stuff! I tell you, if it don't light your fire, then your wood's wet! Everlasting, do you realize what that means? We make cow deals all of the time, and sometimes they hold up pretty good, but everlasting? The Lord is willing to make a deal with you *He* will *never* back out of. You ever done that good on a trade? Listen to this part." He found his place again.

"Seek ye the Lord while *He* may be found, call on *Him* while *He* is near. Let the wicked forsake his way, and the unrighteous man his thoughts and let him return unto the Lord and *He* will have mercy on him; and to our God for *He* will abundantly pardon.

"I really like that part. We're all sinners, me as bad as anybody, but no matter what we've done, we will be forgiven."

An old cowboy stood up in front. "Preacher, if we be counting up noses on sinners, I reckon I shape up to be one of the worst, but I reckon I know it. Can you do something for me?"

"No, cowboy, I can't do anything except help you see where to go for help. If you believe in the Lord, and you believe *He* sent *His* Son to die for your sins, and if you believe Jesus was resurrected and reigns with *His* Father on high, then all you have to do is drop down on your knees right now and ask *Him* to save you and *He'll* do it, right here and now."

The old cowboy was crying openly. He didn't bother to wipe off the tears. "I reckon I do believe, Preacher. I've read in the Book a lot over the years, only I figured I was too far gone. I figured it was too late."

"It's never too late, cowboy. Come down here and offer yourself to God and start a new life."

"What do I say to you?"

"You don't say anything to me, you've already said enough to make me shout Hallelujah and start singing at the top of my lungs. You do your talking now to God."

The cowboy got on his knees, and the preacher said, "I do feel like singing. Does everybody know Just as I am? Let me see your hands if you do." Not many hands went up. "How about 'Rock of Ages'?" A bunch of hands went up, so he started singing. More cowboys got up and came down where the preacher stood. It was a sight to see.

The food was great. The pies were savored to the last bite. Here and there you could see a cowboy actually licking their plates. Then an amazing thing happened. Several people came up to Brother Graham and said, "Preacher, it's been a long time since we heard a good sermon. Some of us wonder, well, if it ain't asking too much, could you come and rip us off another one?"

An encore! Not something preachers get to do often. Back home, the congregation started squirming when he ran a few minutes past the allotted time. This time he chose Psalm 51 as his text and talked about the remission of sins.

After the service a young storekeeper and his wife came up. "Preacher, we're considered married in the eyes of the town, we've posted the banns and all, but we ain't had nobody to do it all legal-like. Is it possible for you to set things straight? Is it too late?"

"The Lord knows what's in your heart, my friend, and *He* knows allowances have to be made in the wilderness. I assure you upstairs Angels are rejoicing with you as we bless your marriage in *His* eyes."

Then came the christenings, four of them. Then people started deciding in favor of baptism, and he waded into the stream and dealt with a whole line of them. He even heard a couple of confessions from Catholics since there were no priests around.

People stayed and stayed and stayed. He was asked a third time to preach, and he did. This time he preached on the Beatitudes, a gentler presentation. The crowd seemed scarcely smaller.

Finally, as people drifted off, the little group was resting by the fire. They looked exhausted. Janie said, "Reverend, you outdid yourself."

"Thank you, Janie, but I think we all know to whom the victory belongs today. You ladies brought them here. You even pointed me towards the words that needed to be said. You have handed me the greatest day in my entire ministry. I shall be grateful for the rest of my life."

"Well, let's just say we all helped," she said, looking around the group, "but all we really did was to set the stage, and God took it from there."

"How very true."

Sixteen:

The Gunfight that Almost Was

Rick rode into Tascosa in a cloud of dust that came up to Sundown's knees. The Texas Panhandle was flat and dry, and there wasn't a tree to be seen for miles, only the tall, blowing grass. The road itself was powdery dirt.

Tascosa was a cow town, wild and wooly and never curried below the knees. The town itself was a small collection of adobe structures and a few slapped up plank buildings. The main street was dirt with several hitching posts. There seemed to be no activity in town except at the Equity Bar, so Rick tied up in front of it.

He smiled at the gentlemen at the bar as he approached and ordered a sarsaparilla, waiting for the usual jokes at his expense because of the order. Instead, one of the men said, "You're that writin' feller, ain't ya?"

"Why yes, I am. I'm Rick Dayton. I write under the name of Texas Jack."

"I thought so. I seen ya in Big Spring."

"Well, my goodness, who would have thought it?"

"Aw, the West is a mighty big place, but everybody pretty much knows everybody else."

"Well, not everybody. I don't know who you are."

"Sorry, I'm Mike Tolbert. I ride for the XIT." He went on to call out the names of others around the room.

"So, how is it people all know each other in such a big land?"

He took a sip of his lukewarm beer and wiped the foam with the back of his hand. "Fer starters, how'd you know to come in here when you rode up?"

"It's where everyone was."

"Exactly. There's over 20,000 square miles here in the panhandle but only three towns, and just one place folks gather in each of them. When we're here, one of the main things we talk about is who we seen where and what they wuz doing. When we camp out on the prairie we can see anybody's campfire for twenty, thirty miles and just natcherly wonder who it is. So, you see if anybody is around, we generally know it, and pretty much know what they're up to.

"Well, I'll be."

"I 'spect you're here hunting another story."

"Yes, that's true."

"Well this place is plumb full of them. There's the story about how the XIT ranch was made up from land given to them in exchange for building the state capitol building. It's a big place, makes up might near half the panhandle."

"That's interesting."

"Don't light your fire, huh? How about Frenchy McCormick? She's a real mystery hereabouts. Get her to tell you her life story and everybody would really be interested. Or...or...I got it. Billy the Kid comes here a lot, there a bunch of guys can tell you stories about him."

"No, I just interviewed him and wrote a book on it."

"No kidding? Say, I gotta read that. Say, what's the matter with me? There's gonna be a big shootout here as soon as Clyde Jenkins hits town. He sent word he's coming. He's looking to take Clay Dunsten down."

"Who's Clay Dunsten?"

"That's him at that back table, drinking alone. Wanna meet him?"

"I'd like that."

They walked over to the man at the table. He was a heavyset man beginning to hang over his belt significantly. He had a black Stetson pushed back slightly, a round face, and he stared at his drink solemnly.

"Clay, this here writing feller wants to meet up with you. His name is Texas Jack."

He looked up. He had a haunted look in his eyes. "I heard about you. Have a seat."

"Actually, my name is Rick Dayton. Texas Jack is a pen name."

"You here for the fight?"

"No, just passing though. Mike told me what was going on."

"You get a reputation with a gun and they never let you be."

"I've heard that. Ace Deadmon told me about it."

"I know Ace. Good man with a gun. He'd know."

"Is he better than you?"

"Wouldn't care to find out. Don't expect I'll get the chance, anyway."

"What's the matter?"

"I figure this to be my last fight. Clyde Jenkins is fast, and I'm not as quick as I used to be."

"So don't fight him."

"It ain't that easy. Once you get a name they keep coming. The ones that won't face you will shoot you in the back the way they did Hickok. They just want to be able to say they was the one that done you in. Ain't no such thing as quitting."

"Maybe, and maybe not. You open to a suggestion?"

"No disrespect, but you don't look like you got the whiskers to be somebody I need to listen to."

"What do you have to lose? Hear me out, then decide."

He listened, then went with Rick over to the newspaper office. He said it was worth a try.

Jenkins hit town and went straight to the Foster and Dunn Saloon for a drink. He knew Clay would be at the Equity and sent word they were to meet in an hour. The time flew, and as the two men stepped out of the respective establishments to face each other across the dusty street Dunsten wasn't wearing a gun.

Jenkins was puzzled. His consternation increased when Rick left the Equity and walked over to him. "You're that writer feller," he declared as he approached.

"Yes, I'm Rick Dayton."

"Ain't the name I heard. I'm gonna give you a big story to write real soon now if you'll get outta the way."

"There's been a small change. Mr. Dunsten has retired from the pistol business."

"Retired? Ain't no such thing. He's just turned yellow." The street was lined with spectators listening to the exchange. He smiled at them, enjoying the exposure. He was a small, slim man, and his dark skin and black moustache gave him a feral look.

"No, he's faced enough men that I doubt anybody would question his courage."

"Well I'm questioning it. I figure he's turned lily-livered, and ain't got enough man left in him to face up to me. But it ain't gonna do him no good. I'm serving notice. I'm gonna count to twenty, and if he ain't strapped on a gun by then I'm gonna shoot him where he stands. That's a time-honored challenge among shootists, and I'm holding him to it."

"I don't think it's going to happen like that, my friend. If you'll look, those boys are handing our circulars announcing Mr. Dunsten's retirement. You'll be pleased to note that in it he concedes the fact that he's just not fast enough any more to match draws against someone of your extreme skill and acknowledges your current superiority publicly and in writing. The document is signed and attested to, and will make quite a keepsake for all of these people."

"It ain't gonna save him."

"I think it will. Since he is unarmed and has made this public statement, it would make it cold-blooded murder to draw on him. Sheriff Jim East and his deputy are holding shotguns on you right at this moment, and in the light of this document would not hesitate to cut you down if you tried to draw on him. Besides, you've gotten what you came for. Not many men have a written testimony from their adversary this way."

"It don't seem right."

"It would if you'd think about it. You're going to want to quit someday yourself. Your reflexes will slow and your eyes will dim, just like Clay's have. Would you like to be able to quit or are you going to insist on being killed?"

"Well, if you put it like that..."

"It's a good deal. You get the benefit without having to—"

"Jenkins!"

The little man spun, pulling his Colt as he turned. A young man leveled his pistol on him. Both guns fired almost as one and both men fell. Rick knelt by his side. "A backshooter, wouldn't you know? Had his gun already on me and I still got him."

"I never saw anything so fast," Rick admitted.

"He got me good, though. I reckon he's killed me. Did I get him?"

Rick looked over at Sheriff East. He was placing the boy's hat over his face and motioning for some bystanders to come carry him. "Yes, you got him."

"Ain't how I figured it'd be. You gonna write about me in your book?"

"You'll be the hero. I think I'll call it *The Gunfight that Almost Was.*"

"That's good. People won't forget me that way." He let out a long sigh, and Rick knew he was gone.

"That's a shame," Clay said from behind him. "I think you reached him." He held out the circular. "You think this worked? I mean, it was your talking that did it this time, how about the next time?"

"You have to keep that gun in a drawer, but yes, I think it'll hold. This story is going to be told, not just in my book, but in newspapers and saloons all over the West. And the heart of the story is the retirement of Clay Dunsten. You stick with it, it'll work."

Seventeen:

Trying Their Wings

Rick's new book was coming along nicely. He had a number of the little dime novels in publication now and could afford to spend the time working on it. He had just been discussing its potential with his horse when he saw an interesting sight ahead of him. He rode towards it.

A young man was lying in the shade beside a small waterhole. It was a hot day and it looked inviting. He rode up and said, "Good morning."

The young man's attention was on a small nest with some young birds in it. The boy started to get up, but Rick stopped him. "Don't get up. My name's Rick Dayton. Mind if I join you?"

"I'm Jeremy. I'm supposed to be cleaning out this waterhole, but I'm afraid I got caught up watching those birds." Jeremy appeared to be maybe ten or twelve. He had carrot-colored hair and was missing some front teeth that made each *S* that he pronounced sound more like *th*.

"Birds?" Rick said, pronouncing the *S* with

difficulty after his example. It wouldn't do to have him think he was mocking him.

"Finches. There's a nest right there with four little ones in it. They're trying to learn to fly. It really caught my eye. I'd like to be able to say I'd seen them do it, fly for the first time, that is. I guess it's a juvenile thing to do. There are times when I think I'm growing up, then I turn around and do something to prove I'm still a kid."

Rick stepped down and lay beside the young man. They got very still.

"There's nothing to be ashamed of in liking wild life or flowers or such, and the young have no corner on curiosity. We can learn a lot from nature. Tell me what's been going on."

"Well, see there? The bird with the bright red head and chest is the daddy. He comes by and encourages them to fly. And here comes mama, she don't have no bright colors. She'll feed them now." He pointed. "See, there are four little mouths open. Two chicks are larger than the other two, and they seem to get most of the food. Those two bigger ones have spent the whole time I've been watching them pruning their feathers, then they get up on the edge and try out their wings. I figure each time they're gonna jump off, but they look down and lose their nerve. The smaller ones don't seem to be interested in anything but eating."

"I see what you mean. You're very observant."

"Poppa and mama and sometimes several others

will come over and hover and yell encouragement at them. They get so excited I think they're going to do it for sure, but they chicken out again."

"Chicken? I thought you said they were finches?"

"Right now they act more like chickens."

"I believe you're right. Look at that little fellow. He's going to do it this time for sure. He wants to do it very badly." The two weren't even aware they were holding their breath as the watched the little bird. Then they exhaled. "Ah, afraid he lost his nerve."

They stayed there watching for a couple of hours. Both of them wanted very much to say they had seen a baby bird take its first flight. Jeremy said, "I feel real guilty about taking the time to do this."

"Some things are simply worth doing. Like stopping to watch the sun rise or set, or watching a baby fawn walk with his mother. Having feelings and liking pretty things doesn't make you any less a man. Besides, as I said, you can learn a lot from nature. You learning anything out of this?"

"I don't know. Like maybe it's hard to leave home for the first time?"

"Is it?" Rick gave him a searching look.

"Yes," he admitted quietly.

"I take it you have left home?"

"Yeah, my pa died. He was all I had left. Mr Jorgenson give me this job."

"I see."

"They look down and it's so far. They're afraid to

try, afraid they'll fall. But their folks keep showing them the way and keep building up their confidence."

"We talking about birds, or are we talking about you? Are you afraid to fall?"

"I guess it's more like I'm afraid to fail. It's safer to just not try, but I guess people have been building up my confidence, too."

"On the first flight, these chicks are probably going to fall."

"I guess so."

"But the bird will get up and will learn fast, or will die. Nature is a difficult taskmaster."

"Yeah, it's kinda tough right now, but I reckon I ain't in any danger of dying."

"All of us have tough times now and then. The secret to being a man is not how many times you get knocked down, but how many times you get back up."

"Maybe nature does have something to teach us. But, I can't stand this any longer. I've got to get back to work. I'm not earning my keep."

"I suppose you're right. There are some things in life that aren't meant to be...wait a minute, that one's all excited, let's give them one more chance."

"Here comes poppa."

"Oh, he's gonna do it...there he goes! Look at that little outlaw go!"

"He didn't exactly fall, but he didn't exactly fly, either."

Rick looked at his grinning face. This would fit

nicely into my book on pioneer lifestyle. "He had those wings going like a hummingbird, though, didn't he? Well, he's committed now. He's got to learn or die. There he goes again."

They watched as the little bird tried again and again, doing a little better each time. Then he made it up to a branch of the tree and rested.

Jeremy said, "That was a bunch of wing flapping for his first ever effort. I bet he's tired."

"Yeah, but he's a bird now. His life just changed completely. It'll never be the same again. Just like losing your dad, we can't undo some things once they're done."

Jeremy nodded and said, "Thanks."

"I should be thanking you. I enjoyed it. How about I help you finish up cleaning out that waterhole?"

Eighteen:

The Fire

"Are you as thirsty as I am, Sundown?" Rick smiled as he gave the horse a pat on the neck. Sundown shook his head as if he understood. "Then I suppose we should alter our course for that windmill on the rise there. It's turning, so it must indicate the availability of water."

A ride of another thirty minutes brought them into hailing distance of the house. The small board building looked out of place in its stark surroundings. He called, "Hello the house!"

"Hello yourself. Come around to the front if you're of a mind."

Rick turned the corner of the house to find a frail, white haired woman sitting in a rocker on the porch. He caught his breath, she reminded him so much of his grandmother. He missed her very much and the pain came unbidden to him. He smiled a sad smile and shook it off.

This lady was peeling potatoes. He removed his hat and said, "Afternoon, ma'am, my name is Rick

Dayton, and I'm seeking water for my animal and myself."

"Well, step down then, and put that hat back on before the sun fries your brains."

"Yes, ma'am."

"You can put your horse in the lean-to and take a bucket water to him. Then come sit a spell and I'll give you a little fresh lemonade."

"That sounds refreshing. I'm surprised you have lemons, however."

"My son brought them back from down on the border. He drives a freight wagon."

"Excellent. I'll return as quickly as I can."

"Fine...and you'll find a cantankerous old rascal by the name of Homer there, most likely asleep leaning against a pitchfork. Might as well bring him back with you."

"Yes, ma'am."

They returned to find the drink sitting by a straight back chair as promised. Rick took a seat. "I'm afraid I didn't catch your name, ma'am."

"Most likely because I didn't say. Folks around here just call me Grandma. Tate, if you gotta have a last name."

"I'm honored, ma'am."

"Danged if you ain't the politest feller I ever met. Makes me a mite nervous."

"I'm sorry, I don't intend to."

"Don't worry, it's kind of a nice change."

He looked at the old man. "And, Homer you are..."

She answered for him. "Hired hand. My man's gone, but I got three growed sons around. Told you about the one that works for the freight line, the other two work on area ranches, but they stop by regular. Once or more will be here every day or two. Homer lives here, but he does day work around, too."

"So you are alone way out here a lot of the time?"

"It ain't so bad. I'm used to it. Emmett, that's my late husband, he hauled freight, too, so he was gone a lot. Was a little harder when we first come out here. Wasn't used to it then. Say, how come you ask so many blame fool questions?"

"I'm sorry, I'm a writer. I collect stories I can use in my books."

"Stories, eh? Used to tell my sprouts lots of stories. Was about the only entertainment we had. Used to make 'em up, I did. Lot's of time out of pretty ordinary stuff, only I spruced 'em up a little to make them more exciting fer the kids."

"I'd love to hear one."

"No kidding? Why I haven't done any storytelling in years. Might be kinda fun."

"Would you mind if I made notes?"

"Notes? You mean you'd use them?"

"I might, with your permission, of course."

"I'd like that. I mean for somebody else to get a little pleasure out of one of my stories." She took a long drink and leaned back in her chair.

"It had been a hot, dry summer and the whole dadblamed prairie looked dead and rattled in the wind. The ranchers all had long faces and a gloomy outlook. They knew if their cows didn't get green grass to graze on soon, they'd be in big trouble.

"We didn't worry about that none, since we didn't have no cows. Actually, I was more interested in the new clothesline Emmett had put up the day before. I was happily rubbing our clothes on the rub-board. I rinsed them, and was about to pin them up on the line when I heard a rumble from the north side of the house. I dropped the shirt back in the basket and run around to have a look.

"I saw a wagon loaded with barrels coming full tilt along the road. A man was standing up in the wagon and was whipping his mules into a belly-down run with a long snake whip. I knew the wagon belonged to the ranch that bordered our little homestead, so I walked up the road a piece to see what was wrong.

"The mules had begun to lather up, so he pulled them down to a walk to let them fetch a breath. He looked over and shouted, 'Prairie fire, miss, on the south range and headed this way!'

"I looked to where he pointed, and sure enough could see the yellow looking smoke off in the distance. He said if it got close enough for me to see the fire, I was to get our belongings and get out.

"Now, I was frantic, I don't mind telling you. I

turned first one way and then the other. How could I take anything with me...alone and on foot? To steady myself, I decided to finish my washing. When I got done, I took the water and spread it on the grass out front. After all, it had to be emptied somewhere, and maybe it would help.

"The smoke kept getting closer, and I went in to see what to take. We really didn't have nothing, no money for sure, so I packed a change of clothes, got the Bible and the family pictures and packed them in a basket by the door. I sure hated to leave my little house. We had worked so hard for what little we had...it just wasn't fair!

"But I did have a plan now. I would go east to the creek. It was almost dry, but the sandy banks offered the only protection I could think of. As I thought, more riders and more wagons went by. I couldn't make out the words, but the gestures and tone was plain enough. 'Prairie fire! Get going!'

"The breeze coming in over the fire was very hot, so my clothes dried quickly. I folded them and took them in the house. I never left my clothes pins out to get dirty, so I gathered them, too.

"Now, I could see some tiny flames once in a while in the yellow-white smoke. I said to herself, when it got to a certain place I would go. Wild pigs, antelopes, and rabbits began to run by on their way to the river, so I figured to get going, too. I boiled up the remaining four eggs in the house, put crackers, cheese, and a can of milk in the basket and prepared to go.

"I can't tell you how alone I felt. I'm afraid I cried as I got my shawl and bonnet and picked up the basket. Would Emmett be worried? Would he find me when he came home tonight? I closed the door behind me...maybe for the last time!

"I walked a good ways before I began to notice how still and stagnant the air was. Ashes began to float down and settle on me. I could see the flames rushing along the ridge that rose south of the house, but the smoke was no longer coming toward me! My heart leaped in my chest.

"At first there was just a tiny movement of air...then a little breeze sprang up from the north, and the fire swung to the west of our house. What a close call! I was so relieved that I sat in the shade of the house, ate my lunch, and said a little prayer for my good fortune."

"What a terrific story." Rick finished his notes. "I wonder what started the fire?"

"Could be most anything, lightning, careless campfire...lots of things," Grandma said.

Homer said, "Yeah, it could be, but it weren't."

She looked at the old man is if she had forgotten he was there. "That's right, you were working over at the LX the day of the fire."

"Shore was!"

Rick turned to a new page. "Mind telling me what happened?"

"Don't mind a-tall. You see, that summer the grass was almighty dry, and when it's like that it don't take much for a fire to get going. Like she said, somebody gets careless with a campfire, or throws down a cigarette, or a bolt of lightning hits, and we got a fire on our hands that can burn thousands of acres.

"I was working the roundup for 'em. We was doctoring some critters that had some kind of skin disease. We were trying to get them treated before they spread it to the rest of the herd."

"How did you treat it?" This was exactly the sort of details Rick wanted to feature in his big book on pioneers.

"The only thing anybody knows will work is to douse it with kerosene. We boxed them in the little chute there, and sprinkled them with a watering can like you'd water flowers. We'd already done a bunch. Those in the pen were the last.

"Just down from us some other hands were doing the branding. Suddenly this old cow we wuz turning loose broke at a crazy angle coming out of the chute and ran right over the branding fire. It became a living torch and ran bawling away."

"Oh my goodness." Rick's writing became frenzied. "What did you do?"

"We shucked our guns and tried to chase the critter down and put it out of its misery. Fore we could catch it, though, it ran by the treated herd and twenty-two balls of fire went running panic stricken in as many directions through the waist high grass.

"It was sumthin' to see. Cowboys ran for their horses and chased steers trying to shoot them before they suffered further. Fire was spreading all over the place and other hands ran for the chain drags to try to stop it before it spread, but it was too late. The cows were lighting a huge area. We were in for the fight of their life.

"We didn't have to send for help. Anyone who saw the smoke would come riding hard, and the smoke could be seen forty, fifty miles away. We just went to work. There was a right smart wind, as usual, and it was spreading the fire rapidly. And the strangest thing, them little dry cow piles that's all over the place, they began catching on fire, and because of their nice round shape would blow in the wind. That really spread the blaze.

"We finished putting them cows out of their misery and came back to help the hands already fighting the blaze. Two teams of men had wet a bunch of hides and were using the chain drags. Behind them men were using sacks, brooms and saddle blankets trying to put out hot spots."

"What are drags?" Rick needed details.

"Just wet hides, weighted with chains, but I gotta tell you they're tough on horses. We'd ride down the leading edge of the fire with one horse inside and one outside of the fire line. This meant the inside horse was running on the burned stubble. We couldn't do that for over a half hour without relief or it'd burn the horse's feet. Then, too, the horses didn't handle the smoke well and got winded easy.

"Some hands arrived from the XIT and the T-Anchor range. With no more chain drags available, they halved the carcasses of the burned cows and began to use them for a drag tying rope to the front and back legs. When it came time for cowboys to rest their mounts they got whatever they could put their hands on and fought fire on the ground.

"There was no rest and no eating during a fire cause we could lose everything we'd gained in minutes. So we fought the fire all night long and well into the next day. Help kept arriving and new lines of battle were set up. Spent horses were rotated out and fresh horses mounted. Remudas were brought up from the BS ranch and from three others.

"Close to sunup the wind died down, and at that point we knew we were winning. Within a couple of hours it was beaten. Some of the newer arrivals began patrolling, looking for any remaining spots still burning. The rest of us drug ourselves back over to the windmill and dropped in our tracks. We were plumb exhausted. I reckon fighting fires or maybe cutting hay are the worst things a cowboy can have to do."

"That's quite a story, from both your perspectives. If you will allow me I shall include it in a book I am doing on pioneer lifestyles. I shall call the chapter 'The Menace of the Deadly Fire.'"

"Isn't that a little much?"

"I'm a professional, I know about these things. I shall put your name on it as told to Texas Jack Hammer."

"Who's he?"

"Me, I am he. It's a name I write under."

"Well, I declare."

Nineteen:

I Been Working on the Railroad

Rick topped the rise and looked down into the small valley. There was a peculiar cloud of dust with a pair of rails extruding from it leading back to the horizon, straight as an arrow. There seemed to be activity within the dust cloud.

"Sundown, I'd say this bears investigating." He turned the big horse's head down the hill and the animal immediately struck up a trot. As Rick got closer he saw it was a railroad crew and they were laying track. Now that would be interesting material for a book.

As he approached a small man walked out a few paces and gave him an appraising look. He looked Rick over so thoroughly he felt that he'd been taped and measured. As he pulled Sundown up, the man said, "Can I h'ep ya?"

"My name is Rick Dayton."

"I be Snooker O'Green. I'm the straw boss of this outfit. What can I do for you?"

"I'm a writer. I had thought there might be a story

to be had here."

"We don't have no use for writers. This be a working camp."

"How about if I sign on for a while, learn what railroad building is all about?"

"Ain't hiring. And no offense, but you don't look to be able to pull your weight if I was hiring."

"I wouldn't expect to be paid."

"Are you daft? You ride up here and ask to do the toughest, meanest job the good Lord saw fit to put on the face of the earth and you don't even want to be paid for it? You ride on out of here afore I take a pick handle to you. I don't cotton to having no looneys around."

"Looneys? Oh, I see, you think I'm crazy. No, I know I wouldn't be much use to you, being the fine physical specimen that I am, but you see I could make my money out of the story I would write about the experience."

"You don't say? Make money for just writing words down? Ain't that a kick in the head? I like to read. Never occurred to me people was making money writing them things. It should have, I guess."

"So how about it?"

"I guess if you're crazy enough to do it, then I'm crazy enough to let you. You got any books with you? I done read everything I got a dozen times."

"I have several of my books. I'll give them to you. You want me to sign them for you?

"If you put your name in them, then they wouldn't be my books, now would they?"

"Of course they would, that's just an author autographing...oh, never mind. Here's a couple of my new ones."

"Say, thanks. You're all right. Who is this Texas Jack feller?"

"That's me. It's the name I write under."

"What fer? You ashamed of your regular name? Or are you a wanted man. No, never mind, sorry I said that. That ain't a question we ask out here. Half my crew is probably wanted back East."

He motioned over a small man wearing granny glasses and red suspenders. "Shortstack, take this here feller over to end of track and see if you can get any work outta him. Try not to hurt him none cause he ain't even on the payroll."

"How'd that come about?"

O'Green walked the little man off a few paces. Shortstack looked Rick's way a couple of times and kept shaking his head. When he came back he treated Rick with the diffidence reserved for the mentally infirm. He shook his head again as he said, "Come with me."

The sun was lowering in the sky before Rick returned. Jumping down from a flatcar on the work train sent a searing pain through his entire body. A whole day of driving spikes with a nine-pound hammer had taken its toll. The fifty yards to the tent looked like an impossible task.

Kelly clapped him on the back and he nearly went to his face. "Let's get washed up and get to the cook shack 'fore Shawn puts it all away."

"Eat? I can't eat. I'm dying. How do you guys do this day in and day out? Every muscle in my body hurts."

"Ahh, me bucko, it's all in what ye be used to. Me, I cou'na ride on me backside chasing cows all day. Glory be but it would be the end o' me."

"Shawn has th' right of it. I like the feel of good honest sweat running down m' back. The free, easy swing of me hammer stretching my muscles and making me feel alive. Trap me behind a desk and I'd die. Suffocate...I swear I would."

Rick looked at the little oriental sitting quietly smoking his pipe. Skinny as Rick was next to the bigger men, he was a head taller and much heavier than the little man. Yet, he had outworked Rick all day, doing the same heavy labor as these huge men, seemingly without effort. He looked up as Rick spoke his name. "Lee chin, I'm bigger than you are, how do you do it?"

The word they apply to the Oriental is inscrutable, with reason. He gave no clue with his face as he formed a reply. "Ah so. I do not fight with the hammer to see who must do the work. Many use muscle and bone to pound the stakes. I use the weight of the hammer and use my body only to start that weight in motion. The arc of the swing does the rest. It only remains for me to guide it through truly to the target."

"So that's it!" Shawn exploded. "Saints preserve us, but I've wondered how the little heathen could match me blow for blow, and here I be twice his natural size if I'm a pound."

Rick worked hard to restrain a smile. "So why haven't you asked him about it?"

"Asked him about it?" He looked at his friend. "Kelly, why haven't we asked him about it before?"

"And why would I be doing that? Me with me fine nose for minding me own business. I be thinking if he'd wanted me to know he'd be about telling me."

"Aye, that would be the straight of it."

"Real men don't ask? Is that it?"

"Well, it'd be like admitting...no, what I mean to say is it would seem like...*Blast it all*, I don't know what I mean, but it wouldn't be right."

"But now that you know?"

"Saints alive, I'd not be above learning a little something from any man and if he'd be of a mind to show how to make this hammer do the work for me..."

The inscrutable face broke into a toothless grin. "I show. You will see. It is easy."

They strode off to the cook shack, loud and boisterous. Rick sat on his cot and started the notes for his new book in the journal. He hoped to be able to catch the rich texture of this camp. The smell, the look of these men, the feel of the camaraderie among them exuded power and manliness. His eyes began to get heavy. Maybe some sleep. He had no idea how he was going to be able to do it again, but he was going to have to try, not because he needed to prove anything to them, they accepted him at face value. No, he needed to prove something to himself, and he was determined that he would be able to do it.

Twenty:

The Dancing Lesson

Rick stopped on the rise overlooking a small colony. The inhabitants of the Texas Panhandle called it Saint's Roost, but the given name was Clarendon.

He wrote the name in his journal along with a little description he had learned from Grandma Tate"

The town site was on a flat where Carroll Creek entered the Salt Fork of the Red River. A road was leading over a bluff to the Northeast going to Mobeetie and Fort Elliott, and another out over the caprock escarpment to the Northwest where it would traverse the plains to Tascosa. These were the only two other towns in the panhandle.

In the center of town was the first building the people had built, a one-room frame building which served as a combined church and school. Most towns out this way built around a saloon or railhead, so this (along with the fact that the town was established by a group of Methodist ministers) had given rise to the name "Saint's Roost."

Now the population had risen to about 400 so-called Saints and assorted buffalo hunters. Homes were spread out along Carroll Creek.

The most substantial structure was a rock hotel managed by a German by the name of Hefflebower. The remainder of the commercial district was comprised of a blacksmith shop, a wagon yard, and a general store. A boot maker's shop was located a little further down the street, and amazingly enough a man by the name of Seman Tabor had a substantial orchard and garden going and was the only green grocer within 100 miles.

Rick rode into town. Looking around, he asked a man on the sidewalk where the nearest saloon was, knowing that would be the most likely place to find a story.

"The saloon? Ain't you heard? Clarendon is drier than the dust in a mummy's pocket. You got to go to Rosie's store fer anything ya need."

So Rosie's it was. There he found out since the character of this town differed so much from the other towns, so did the person of its sheriff. Over in Mobeetie, the sheriff was Cap Arrington, former Texas Ranger and a man of great reputation. In Tascosa, it was Jim East, and he was as wild as was the town. In Clarendon, it was Al Gentry who pinned on the badge. Gentry was southern plantation aristocracy and a graduate of Washington University. He was said to be Goodnight's sheriff, because part of his job was to see the tick-bearing, South Texas cow herds went around the JA Ranch rather than through it.

It didn't take much to get those hanging around the store talking about Gentry.

One lady said, "Well, I like him. He's such a nice man, but he's rather quiet. Do you think he's the type to be a sheriff?"

A freighter who had brought in supplies said, "Shucks, ma'am, Gentry ain't feared of nothing. Didn't you hear what happened in Abilene?"

She shook her head, no.

The man reared back and hooked his thumbs in his suspenders. "Only backed down Wild Bill Hickok, that's what."

"You're kidding!" Her eyes were wide.

"No, ma'am. I been known to stretch the truth a mite if it improves the telling, but this here tale don't need no stretchin'."

He twirled the end of his mustache and looked around his small audience with a twinkle in his eye. Satisfied he had their full attention, he went on.

"Well, Gentry was setting by himself at a table in a saloon, when Wild Bill came in with a bunch of his friends. Now Bill had been lubricating his tonsils, and when he saw this here newcomer sitting there so quiet, he took him for a tenderfoot and undertook to have a little sport at his expense. He pulled out his hardware, ordered him to dance, and went to shooting at his feet.

With a smile he leaned forward to take them all into his confidence. "Well, old Gentry still didn't say a word, and he didn't as much as blink while Hickok blazed away. Bill thought that shined, sure enough, and went over and put his arm around his shoulder and offered to buy him a drink."

He straightened up and raised his voice. "But instead, Gentry shucked his own gun and threw down on Hickok. He said, 'Now, it's my turn. You dance and you do it quick, cause if you don't, I'll not pepper your feet, I'll shoot you stone cold dead.' And Hickok didn't have no choice but to dance. No, if you ask me, I figure your sheriff has got the stuff and plenty of it."

"Well, my goodness," she said. "Who would have thought it?"

Twenty-one:

The Death of Grandmother

Rick stared at the yellow page. The telegram read GRANDMOTHER VERY ILL--STOP--FAMILY CALLED HOME--STOP. It was signed James. James was a cousin, one he had played with as a child.

He must go, of course. He asked the telegrapher/station attendant for a ticket to Boston on the earliest train. It would be the following morning. He would have to make arrangements to board Sundown, settle up at the hotel, store a few things at the freight office...

Rick was burying himself in details to avoid thinking of what was really at the back of his mind, Grandmother Henson. She was the matriarch, the rock the family was built upon. He could scarcely imagine her ill, let alone in serious condition.

The Irish can do guilt, and Rick indulged himself in doing just that all night, sleeping fitfully in between sessions of worry and remorse that he had not been back to see her sooner. He had been too caught up in his own life, his own adventure. Family should be more important. Somewhere in the dark he found enough sleep to finish passing the night.

Rick caught the early train, and found the trip back a blur of day and night, muddled thoughts, trying to write but unable to string coherent words together. His chest was constricted, his head fuzzy, and he did not want to eat. Classic depression. It took years to make the journey...or perhaps only moments...time became irrelevant. In real terms it was but days.

He rushed from the station to grab a carriage and hurry to the house. He found it full of somber faced relations, many of whom he had not seen in years. James intercepted him. "No time to be greeting relatives, Rick. There may not be much time."

"So I'm not too late?"

"The doctor is with her now."

"The telegram didn't say..."

"Cancer. It's advanced. The doctor doesn't hold out any hope. She's in a lot of pain, but I think she's been hanging on waiting for you. She knew you were on the way." James gave him a funny little smile. "It's okay, I've been right here for her, but you've always been her pet."

They were interrupted by the doctor coming out of the room at the head of the stairs. James said, "Doctor, this is Rick."

"Hello, young man, you'd best hurry in. The end is near I fear. Actually, I don't know how she's made it this long."

"There's no hope?"

"She's in terrible pain. I've just given her a big dose of Laudanum trying to make her as comfortable as I could. Still, she can't hang on much longer."

Thanking him, Rick hurried up the stairs. He recognized the smell as he came in the room. Cancer has a sort of sweet, yet stale odor that was unmistakable. He had smelled it before. He hurried to take up her hand. "I'm here, grandmother."

"Rick, is it really you?" She strained to focus, but the medication made it difficult.

"I'm sorry I haven't been here, Grandmother. I feel so bad."

"But you have been here, Rick." She managed a small smile "Or should I say Texas Jack?" She motioned to her bedstand, and he saw all of his books. They looked dog-eared and used. "We have been together each day. You have been my eyes to the world I no longer had the legs to go see. I couldn't have felt closer to you if you had been at my side day and night." She squeezed his hand. It was faint, but he felt it. "We have had such wonderful adventures together."

"You may not believe it, but I felt you there. I thought of you often, and found myself thinking, 'Grandmother would love this'."

"Yes, I do believe it, but I am so glad you got here. I wanted to see you again so badly. I can go now. There has been so much pain, I just can't tell you..."

"I'm sorry you suffered because of me."

"No! Please don't think that. I know you came immediately. Even with such pain one doesn't want to let go. It's hard to say goodbye to life. It's all we know. Still, I have no doubts. I know the Lord is waiting for me, I'm content now to go to Him."

She stiffened up, obviously hit by a huge pain. Rick held her close and whispered in her ear. "Grandmother, I love you so much. I always will. I can't stand to see you suffer like this. Let it go."

Rick felt her relax in his arms and heard a long exhale of breath. She was gone. It hit him like a sledgehammer. What had he done? He told her to leave and she had gone. He had no right...

Rick stumbled out to tell the others. Tears streaming down his face he confessed.

James was crying, too. "She was ready, Rick. You just gave her permission."

"My head tells me that, James, but my heart isn't buying it."

There was nothing left for Rick in Boston. He attended the funeral, then hastened to leave as shortly thereafter as possible. James took him back to the train. "I guess you're eager to get back to your writing. I sure enjoy your books."

"Thank you, but I think I'll be taking some time off. This took a lot out of me. It's as if the funeral absorbed everything I had and left me an empty vessel."

"It'll come back."

"Yes, I'm sure it will, but I won't rush it."

They said their good byes and Rick watched James diminish in the distance as the train left a narrow rail in its wake.

Rick chose a seat. He wondered how long it would take to return to writing, or if he even could. He felt as if he were completely empty. Maybe he had burned out. Perhaps he was truly...

"Hello."

Rick looked up to see a straw hat. Beneath it were two remarkable blue eyes framed between golden pigtails. The memory of his first trip flooded back on him, and intensified when an unseen lady said, "Mandy, you turn around and leave the gentleman alone."

What a remarkable coincidence. Rick found himself thinking everything was going to be all right. In that same instant he knew something else, his grandmother was still with him. He leaned back and smiled. "Grandmother, here we go on another adventure."

Meet the Author:

Terry was an EPPIE Award finalist with "To Keep a Promise" from The Fiction Works and the trade paperback version was nominated for the Willa Award. Other publishing credits include "Don't I Know You?" also from The Fiction Works, both books scheduled from the same publisher in audio in the near future. He has a book of cowboy poetry entitled "Cowboys Don't Read Poetry, from Txjack Publications" and an audio book version of Trails of the Dime Novel" from JBS Publications. His short stories are included in six short story collections including "From the Heart" and "From the Heart 2" from Coastal Villages Press and "Living by Faith" from Obidiah Press. He has a new Christian western series from River Oak Press starting with "Mysterious Ways." He's published over 200 articles and short stories.

"Dime Novel is one of my favorites," Burns said. "It was a fun book from start to finish, and I suppose I identify with the naive young man roaming the west writing the stories. I'm still that young in spirit."

Available now

from

Echelon Press Publishing

Redemption

By

Morgan J. Blake

Chapter One

Superstition Mountains, Arizona Territory–late spring, 1873

"Kinson, you don't want to go up there," Lieutenant Sam Skinner called as he hurried after him.

Wylie Kinson barged up the trail, approaching one of Skinner's young underlings who stood in the narrowest part of the path. With trembling hands, the kid attempted to roll a cigarette. Wylie slowed as he drew near, tipping his rifle's barrel up just a little.

"Move," Wylie barked.

The kid's head snapped up, his eyes wide. When he didn't respond, Wylie stopped directly in front of him. The young private stared at him for a second, then glanced at Skinner.

"Don't you look at him. Look at me. I'm the one orderin' you right now." There was no kindness in Wylie's voice.

"Kinson, don't start with him," Skinner said.

Damn you, Skinner…don't you start with me. *Wylie didn't turn, but stepped even closer to the kid before him, bumping the private in the chest with the rifle. The kid backed up a step, then another, much like an animal ready to turn tail and run.*

"It's alright, Portney. Let him through," Skinner said. At his quiet, disarming words, Portney stepped off the path.

Wylie again hurried on, leaving Skinner to tell the young man to find some shade and rest. He then charged after Wylie.

"Kinson, that was uncalled for."

The officer's words barely registered in Wylie's mind, so intent was he on reaching the outcropping of boulders on the hill above them. Trained as a scout, he normally took great care to notice every detail. Now he walked forward, oblivious to everything around him.

One of the settlers had told Wylie the news that morning when he reached the village. At first, he'd been numb. The farther he rode trying to find the soldiers, the more the numbness gave way to rage. Only now, as he walked toward the hill, did he feel the intense ache, and that only served to anger him more. *Why'd you let this happen, God? Huh?*

Wylie felt neither the warmth from the glaring sun nor the occasional breeze, and was only vaguely aware of the trickle of sweat snaking its way between his shoulder blades. Still, he looked past the boot tracks on the desert floor as if there was nothing there.

Wylie slowed his pace when he reached the foot of the hill and looked up at the cactus-speckled boulders. He studied the steep slope ahead of him, squinting against the day's brightness. Skinner now stood beside him, his jaws flapping like a busted gate in a gale wind, but Wylie paid no heed to the officer. Checking the time by the sun's position, he finally turned back to the hill. He closed his eyes.

I don't want to do this. Shifting his feet on the rocky terrain, he opened his eyes again to squint at the place they'd pointed to moments before. He cursed himself silently with a frustrated shake of his head. *Do it and get it over with. You know you'll never forgive yerself if you stay below and let someone else tend to this business. Ya got enough regrets without adding this one to the list.*

Shifting his rifle between hands, Wylie dried one palm, then the other, on his pant legs. With that, he started forward again.

"Kinson, would you stop?" Skinner called in frustration as he again hurried after Wylie.

Ignoring the officer, Wylie walked ahead a few steps before a new sound stopped him. To the right of the path, a good twenty feet out in a small, bare patch among the ocotillo, cholla, and saguaros, he heard the other soldiers' laughter mingled with the sound of shovels biting into the parched desert floor. The laughter started out hesitantly, with one soldier chuckling at some not-so-funny comment to break the tension, the others following suit.

Wylie watched them with a cold expression. How many times had it been him standing there, laughing like a fool? He glanced at the rocky earth between his boots, noticing a dark stain near the edge of the path. As he bent over and touched his fingers to it, he glared again at the bunch of them. Their banter continued, every one of them oblivious to his stare.

His anger exploding, he jacked a shell into the chamber of his rifle, took aim at the ground between the feet of the nearest man, and fired. The gun bucked hard against his shoulder, the concussion echoing against the rocks.

The bullet hit the edge of the hole they were digging, knocking a chunk of the soil loose, and collapsing the ground under the soldier's foot. With a surprised yelp, he started to fall but caught himself. The others looked up, startled, and quickly ducked out of the way. A couple of them even jumped into the shallow hole they'd dug. Two men below scrambled for their rifles, just out of reach. Wylie covered one of the men.

"Next one of you who think this is funny is likely to wind up with an extra hole in his..."

Skinner dashed in front of Kinson, arms up as he hollered out for all to hear.

"Stop this! Now!"

The soldiers below stared up at the two of them, a mix of expressions on their faces. Seething, Wylie glared down at them, his rifle still poised at his shoulder.

Skinner turned on him. "Put the gun away, Kinson. Are you trying to get yourself killed?" he stormed.

His commanding voice lent an air of importance and control to his demeanor. Again, he swung around to face his soldiers.

"Get back to work now."

Like shamefaced children scolded by an angry father, the soldiers set to work without the banter, squirming under Wylie's attention.

Satisfied they would no longer make light of the situation, Wylie lowered the gun and shifted his attention to the stained ground. He couldn't be sure, but it was an easy guess to assume the spot was dried blood. Wylie studied it for only an instant before he started to move again, heading toward the hill. As he reached the base, Skinner hurried around in front of him.

"Kinson, stop," the officer commanded, placing a restraining hand on Wylie's shoulder.

Wylie bristled. He turned on Skinner and brushed his hand away before he stepped around the officer.

"I'll thank you to stay out of my way," he growled.

"Wylie–!" Skinner grabbed his arm.

Wylie stiffened at the contact, then turned to face the lieutenant.

"Who do you think you are, Skinner? Damn you, that's my

mother up there!"

His voice softened when he spoke again. "Kinson, let someone else handle it. You don't want to see her like this."

Wylie prepared to pounce. "What if it was Jaylene up there?" Wylie challenged. "Wouldn't you want to see your *wife*?"

After a moment's hesitation, Skinner responded in a quiet voice.

"I know you're still angry, Kinson...."

"You're damn right I'm angry," Wylie interrupted, taking a step closer to Skinner until he towered over the shorter man. "You cost me the woman I love."

Skinner took a slow step backwards and answered in a gentle tone. "No, friend, you lost her yourself."

Wylie glared at Skinner, wanting very much to plant his fist into that innocent face of his, but the truth of Skinner's statement kept him from it. His own stupidity *had* lost him Jaylene, and getting into a fight with her husband wouldn't change that fact. Besides, there were other, more important things to tend to.

"One thing we're not and never will be is *friends*. Now get out of my way."

Wylie's demeanor dared Skinner to challenge him, but when Skinner didn't move, Wylie shifted his rifle in his hands and started up the slope.

The sound of the shovels slowed, then stopped behind him as he climbed up the rocky steepness. Instinct told him that every man in the camp was watching him. *Is this how it's gotta be, God? Every man down there watchin' what oughta be a private matter? Well, to hell with all of 'em.* He squared his shoulders and continued forward. Yet for all his brash thoughts, he still wished they would mind their own business.

He studied the ground, finding a drop of blood here, a partial boot print a little farther onward. Continuing up the steep hill, he saw a bloody handprint, far too small to belong to a man. He hesitated there, kneeling near the print so he could study it in detail. Wylie touched the stained earth, covering the bloody handprint with his own larger hand. The earth was hot under his touch, so hot he wanted to draw his hand away. He didn't move.

What did they do to you, Ma? Who are these bastards, and what hell did they put you through? Did Cara see it? Have they hurt her or Jaylene? For several minutes, Wylie knelt like that, trying to feel something, trying to understand the struggle that had caused his mother to leave behind her handprint. But when his mind turned to the thought of rape or torture, he pushed himself up.

His insides twisted into a tight knot. An uneasy burn started in the pit of his stomach, just as it had when they first told him of the kidnappings. He realized then just how dry his mouth was. Wylie glanced down, hoping to see his canteen. Not finding it, he realized he'd left it looped over his saddle horn when he dismounted from his buckskin.

He swore under his breath, wiping at the sweat that trickled into his eyes. With a scowl, he started again. Reaching the crest of the hill, he found the hot ground stained dark with more blood droplets. He took off his hat and ran his fingers through his hair, wishing he didn't have to do this. He'd seen death before, held dying men in his arms as their lives seeped away. Until now, it had never been a family member. Wylie steadied himself against the nearest boulder, took a deep breath, then walked around behind the rocks.

Concentrating on his boots, he tried to steel himself for what he had to do. Wylie licked his lips, then looked around the area, avoiding his mother's body for a moment more. Finally, he took a deep breath and turned his attention to the bloodstained earth near her body, then to her face.

Dried blood covered her chin and cheek, and one sightless eye stared up at the afternoon sun. The other eye was gone, having become a feast for one of the first scavenger birds to happen along.

"Aw, hell," he whispered, the word slipping out unheeded. He looked away, pressing his eyes closed against the sight. *Why are You doin' this to me? This is my ma...*

It took him several seconds to shift his attention back to her. When he did, he found raw, bloody flesh where her throat had been cut. Wylie's knees buckled, and he sat down hard, losing his grip on the rifle as he did so. The gun clattered against the ground, but he didn't hear it. He heard nothing but silence.

Wylie pressed his eyes closed and swallowed. Beads of sweat formed on his skin, and he fought hard to force the hot air into his lungs. It was several seconds later when he finally brought himself to look at her again.

Blood mottled the front of her pale blue calico dress, and he could see where more birds had picked at her flesh. Lunging up, Wylie turned away and vomited.

After a moment, he straightened and stumbled to the boulders, leaning his shoulder against the largest one. Dizziness swept over him, but he managed to keep his feet under himself this time. Slowly, he turned toward the path leading back to the others.

"Skinner," he called. His voice sounded strange, almost hollow. He waited for a moment, then called again. Wylie spit into the dirt and wiped the sweat from his forehead.

Finally, Skinner appeared on the path. For a moment, he stood quietly, glancing uncomfortably at the body before settling his attention fully on Wylie.

"Are you alright?" the officer asked in a quiet voice.

Wylie settled his back against a boulder, staring out across the rough, mountainous terrain. Heat waves danced in the distance, obscuring the saguaros and playing tricks on his eyes. He focused on nothing in particular as he tried to force himself to concentrate on why he'd called the other man up the hill. He rubbed his hand over the stubble on his jaws as he thought, then looked at the officer.

"I need something to cover her with. And also my canteen."

"Kinson, you haven't stopped for days. Now that you've seen her, why don't you get some rest? We can take care of things from here. You're going to need your strength and your wits to find Cara. Your sister is counting on you."

"You're not gonna get mouthy again, are you, Skinner?"

There was a long pause before Skinner answered.

"No."

Wylie turned away from him with a quiet word of thanks. From the corner of his eye, he saw Skinner nod once, then disappear.

As he turned to look at his mother's face again, fatigue stole over him. Skinner was right. He needed to rest, but he couldn't. Not until he'd seen to his mother. Wylie moved toward her, fighting the uneasiness in the pit of his stomach.

It had been over three years since he'd last seen her or Cara, years he realized he should not have missed. As he stared at her torn body, Wylie recalled the nights she'd sung him to sleep beside the fire when he was a child, the time that she'd tearfully forgiven both him and Cara after they'd broken the heirloom mirror she'd brought from the East. A sad smile crept onto his face at the thought of the many times she'd sternly, yet lovingly, reprimanded him for finding trouble. This woman had raised him with great care and much love; she'd always been there when he needed her.

But when she and Cara needed him, he wasn't there.

"I didn't mean to disappoint you. I never should've left," he whispered to her.

Hearing a noise, Wylie turned to find Skinner standing a few feet away, a tarpaulin in one hand, canteen in the other. Wylie took a step toward him, motioning for the canteen. Skinner passed it to him without a word.

Pulling off the cork stopper, Wylie drank long of the lukewarm water, then splashed some on his face.

"The men are about done digging the grave, Kinson," he said gently, motioning toward the path.

Wylie looked in the direction of his mother's body, although he couldn't bring himself to look at her.

I don't want to bury you, Ma.

"Alright."

Skinner dropped the tarpaulin before he turned away. He took a hesitant step, then called over his shoulder. "Wylie, I'm very sorry. She was a good woman. Jaylene loved her like..." Skinner's already quiet voice trailed off. Wylie glanced away as the man unabashedly wiped at his eyes. Skinner hesitated another moment, as if he were going to continue, but disappeared behind the rocks without another sound.

Picking up the canvas tarpaulin, Wylie unfolded it and spread it out on the ground beside her body. He sank down to his knees beside her and pulled the bandana from around his neck. Wetting it with the canteen, Wylie cleaned away the dried blood covering her face.

"This is my fault," he whispered to her. "You begged me not to go. You said I was makin' a mistake. I made lots of 'em. That one was just the first. I shouldn't have left. If I'd stayed..." His voice dwindled to nothing. He sucked in a ragged breath, cursing himself and his own stubbornness. "...If I'd stayed, maybe I could have stopped this from happening to you. Maybe you, Cara, and Jaylene would still be at home where ya belong."

He looked down at her, focusing on the wound at her throat. *How dare You let her die this way, God?*

Something about that ragged gash nagged at him; something was not quite right. Tugging his hat a little lower against the bright sunlight, he studied things. The wound was deep, so it should have produced a lot of blood. As he studied it, the nagging idea began to make sense.

"Where's all the blood? The front of your dress is too clean for—" He stopped mid-thought. Turning her body over, Wylie discovered that the back of her calico dress was stained crimson with her blood, and there was a ragged tear in her dress bodice an inch below her right shoulder blade. As the blood had dried in the arid desert air, the fabric stuck to her skin. Wylie cautiously ran his hand over her back, finding a bullet wound hidden under the torn fabric.

"Oh, Ma," he whispered, eyeing the torn flesh. He put his hand over the wound, fighting against the idea of the suffering she'd endured before her death. It was obvious to him now that his mother died from the bullet wound, not from the gash at her throat. But it made no sense. Apaches were known to mutilate their victims. If the Apaches were to blame, they would've likely done more than just this. An Apache would have left her nearly unrecognizable. So who else would do such a thing? Why would someone shoot her in the back, then mutilate her after she was already dead?

With gentle hands, Wylie rolled her over again and tucked his bandana into her hand. Unable to make himself look at her face, he sat for several moments, holding her limp fingers in his.

So many things I needed to say to you, Ma. For so long you watched me squander my life, and for the last three years of that time, I ain't been ready to face you because of it. Ma, I was comin' home to tell you I was ready to pull myself together, quit the Army, and settle down somewhere. But now you ain't ever gonna hear that.

"I'm so sorry, Ma."

With a sigh, he lifted her body onto the tarpaulin. He brushed the hair from her face with a gentle hand, then wrapped her body in the canvas, leaving only her face exposed.

Crouching down beside her, he touched her cheek as fury boiled up from the pit of his stomach. Every muscle in his body went rigid.

"I promise you, I won't rest until Cara and the others are safe, and the bastards who did this to you are dead," he whispered in his mother's unhearing ears.

He licked his lips again as he thought of the other women. Cara and Jaylene, as well as several of their friends, were somewhere out there. He would find them. His only hope was that he could find them in time to prevent their deaths.

"I swear it," he said, looking down at her one last time. "I won't let this happen to Cara."

Experience the thrill of
Echelon Press

The Plot
ISBN 1-59080-203-9

Kathleen Lamarche
$13.49

Pattern of Violence
ISBN 1-59080-278-0

C. Hyytinen
$14.99

Missing!
ISBN 1-59080-204-7

Judith R. Parker
$12.99

The Rosary Bride
ISBN 1-59080-227-6

Luisa Buehler
$11.99

Unbinding the Stone
ISBN 1-59080-140-7

Marc Vun Kannon
$14.99

Redemption
ISBN 1-59080-389-0

Morgan J. Blake
$15.99

Crossing the Meadow
ISBN 1-59080-283-7

Kfir Luzzatto
$11.99

Justice Incarnate
ISBN 1-59080-386-8

Regan Black
$13.99

Drums Along the Jacks Fork
ISBN 1-59080-308-6

Henry Hoffman
$11.99

The Last Operation
ISBN 1-59080-163-6

Patrick Astre
$13.49

To order visit
www.echelonpress.com
Or visit your local
Retail bookseller

Printed in the United States
24507LVS00001B/226-285